The Tijuana Bible

Other (but by no means all) books by this author

A Graveyard of My Own
Everybody Comes to Cosmo's
Daredevils, Ltd.
The Great Comic Book Artists
The Great Comic Book Artists, Volume 2
Starpirate's Brain

The Tijuana Bible

Ron Goulart

St. Martin's Press, New York

THE TIJUANA BIBLE. Copyright © 1989 by Ron Goulart. All rights
reserved. Printed in the United States of America. No part of this
book may be used or reproduced in any manner whatsoever
without written permission except in the case of brief quotations
embodied in critical articles or reviews. For information, address St.
Martin's Press, 175 Fifth Avenue, New York, N.Y. 10010.

Design by Karin Batten

Library of Congress Cataloging-in-Publication Data

Goulart, Ron.
    The Tijuana bible.
      p. cm.
    "A Thomas Dunne book."
    ISBN 0-312-03440-7
    I. Title.
PS3557.085T55   1989   813'.54—dc20   89-34942

First Edition

10 9 8 7 6 5 4 3 2 1

The Tijuana Bible

Chapter

1

Although romance and money are undeniably two of the essentials of life, the opportunity to attain sufficient amounts of either often eludes us. For instance, it wasn't until Jack Deacon was very near his thirty-seventh birthday that he got a chance at enough of both.

And that was only because, right at the start of things, the dying man made a mistake.

It had been raining for what seemed like forty days and forty nights in Jack's part of Connecticut and the small studio in his recently rented and not quite big enough cottage felt damp and chill despite the fire trying to crackle in the narrow stone fireplace.

Hunched slightly, the long lanky man was seated at his drawing board in the center of the white-walled room. He was contemplating an absolutely blank sheet of white typing paper and listening to the downspout out on the small night patio slurp and gurgle.

The phone rang.

Jack watched it through a few rings, then picked it up. "Yep?"

"Um . . . Jack. This is Mario."

"Who?"

"Mario DaVinci . . . from the Brimstone Trust Company . . . your bank."

"These aren't banker's hours."

"No, I . . . well, forgive me, but . . . um . . . I couldn't help overhearing your little argument with Mr. Germeshausen this afternoon."

"Wasn't an argument. I told him to go fuck himself."

"Yes, exactly, but . . . um . . . one doesn't tell Mr. Germeshausen to . . . to do that."

"Did he suggest you phone me? 'Call this Deacon fellow and inform him he can't tell me to go fuck myself.'"

"Oh, no . . . I'm calling you from my home, Jack. . . . One of the reasons is . . . um . . . well, I'm something of a cartoon buff and I admire your work on *Freddie Foible*."

"I only assist on the damn strip."

"Ah, but . . . um . . . I can tell your touch, in the drawings and in the jokes."

"Matter of fact, I have to have ten more daily strip gags to turn into my boss, Wally Warfield, early tomorrow. So if—"

"What I'm . . . um . . . getting at, Jack. I think I might be able to persuade Charlie . . . Mr. Germeshausen . . . to extend your loan another ninety days. Will that help?"

"It will, yes. By then the dough from the sale of the house ought to have come in."

2

"I knew you'd been . . . um . . . having financial difficulties of late and so I—"

"Financial difficulties? My wife cleaned out all our joint accounts and ran off to South America with a sailor. Fortunately the house was in my name or—"

"That's nice, Jack. I see you've kept your sense of humor and can . . . um . . . kid about your adversities."

"I'm not kidding. She did run off with a sailor. And they're in South America. He calls himself a lieutenant commander, but that's still a sailor."

"Why not . . . um . . . after you see Mr. Warfield tomorrow . . . drop in at the bank to see me, Jack?"

"Fine, I will. I appreciate this."

"Would it be all right if I brought a sketchbook of my own drawings and cartoon ideas along to show—"

"Sure, I'd love to look the stuff over." Jack's lean face took on a sorrowful expression, but his true feelings never sounded in his voice. "Thanks again, Mr. DaVinci."

"You can call me Mario."

"Fine. I was going to invite you to call me Jack, but you already are. Let's hope . . . Oops, I have another call coming in, Mario. See you at the bank tomorrow."

He hung up, sighed. "Jesus, I'm being slowly buried in debt and now I have to look at some gay banker's etchings."

He scowled at the sheet of blank paper that ought to have had at least one daily *Freddie Foible* gag on it by now.

"Can senility hit this soon before forty?"

The rain had lost none of its enthusiasm. It pounded on the slanting shingle roof of the studio, hit hard at the high wide windows. Jack, who'd moved into this rented cottage five weeks ago, hadn't as yet gotten

3

around to putting up curtains or drapes. The windows showed him the black wet night.

"Probably very few Peeping Toms are interested in torpid cartoonists anyway."

The cottage sat at the downslant of a sloping five acres. Off through a now-overgrown wooded area, sprawled a big stone house. The owners, his landlords, were off basking in one of the many warmer climes available to people who didn't have to work at assisting cartoonists and whose wives hadn't proved unreliable.

There was also, off there in the darkness someplace, a carriage house, rundown and in disuse.

"Horse," he muttered, turning his attention again to the sheet of paper. He picked up a porous-point pen from the taboret next to his slanting drawing board. "Let's see. Freddie bets on the horses . . . he goes horseback riding . . . he's so hungry he could eat a horse . . ."

Leaning back in his chair, letting his eyelids half-close, Jack scribbled on his thumb with his pen. He drew a daisy and was working on a stem when he heard a shot.

It was a muffled cracking noise, but Jack was certain he'd just heard a gun being fired.

He was out of his chair, loping toward the window. He couldn't see a damn thing out there.

Not at first.

Then the spill of light from his studio showed him a figure, stumbling and weaving, coming toward him. It was as though the pudgy man in the rumpled dark suit was being hauled toward the window on a line.

The light from the windows hit him fully at last as he tripped over the low shrubs and fell against the glass.

His fat fingers spread out across the rain-wet glass, his bloody forehead pressed against a pane.

Jack recognized him. "Mutt Shermer."

The fat man's glazed eyes were staring in from out of the rainy night, yet he didn't seem to be focusing on anything.

Jack made a stay-right-there motion at Mutt, pivoted and ran from the room. He scooted down the hall, slowed and stopped at the closet. He grabbed his tan raincoat, managing to pull down three hangers and a red mackinaw he'd been meaning to donate to the Goodwill.

The rain came slamming down at him as he hit the flagstone path outside his front door.

He'd forgotten he was wearing slippers. His feet turned rapidly wet and chill.

Jack sloshed his way around the cottage, over the threadbare lawn to where Mutt Shermer had appeared.

The pudgy man had slid farther down. He was on his knees, leaning against the wet window panes with his head turned sideways. There was a raw, black-rimmed splotch on his cheek and the night rain was hitting it, making it spurt pale red.

"Mutt, what the hell are you doing out here?"

The older cartoonist moved his head very slowly to look at the crouched Jack. "Where's Sally?"

"Who?"

He wheezed, brushed at the burn on his cheek with his left hand. There were two more raw round wounds on his palm. It looked to Jack like someone had held a lighted cigarette to him.

"You'll have to tell her, Jack," he said.

Leaning closer, Jack slipped an arm around the soggy, disheveled man. "We'll get you inside, buddy, and phone a—"

"Listen to me," said Mutt. "Tell Sally . . . tell her . . . he still had them all . . . timely DC faucet . . ."

"Sure, I'll tell her. Now see if you can maybe walk. Not that far to—"

"He wanted her to have them . . ."

"We'll see to that, sure." He had absolutely no idea who Sally was or what the wounded man was talking about.

"The key to the whole . . . Listen to me, damn it. This is important." He grabbed at Jack's sleeve, caught it, pulled him closer to his cracked lips.

"I can hear you, Mutt."

"The key is . . . the Tijuana Bible."

"What?"

"The Tijuana Bible," he repeated and died.

Jack watched the body for a moment, the rain pelting at it and washing at the wounds, the welts, and bruises.

Then something happened to him that had never happened to him before. He got hit on the head.

He recognized the symptoms immediately. "Hey, I've been sapped," he said to himself.

He started to fall and never felt himself land.

———

His mouth tasted muddy, his tongue felt about an inch or so too wide, jagged pain was roaming through his skull. Jack opened his eyes and for the first seconds saw only zigzags of intensely bright light, a sort of busted kaleidoscope effect.

He was sprawled among the shrubbery, prickly, dull-green stuff he didn't know the name of. The rain was pelting him, needling his back, splashing up mud all around him.

"Mutt Shermer," he remembered, pushing at the gritty ground with both hands.

He made it up to his knees, witnessing another brief but impressive light show.

Jack discovered he was breathing in a different way, in and out through his mouth, panting, dog-style.

6

Lurching, he braced one hand against the faded shingle wall of his cottage. He panted a few more times, then eased himself up to a standing position.

He stayed propped against the side of the house, concentrating on remaining upright, careful not to give in to the impulse to throw up.

Taking a slow look around, he did a take. A cautious take, one that wouldn't jiggle his aching head.

Mutt was gone.

The pudgy man wasn't spread out on the ground any longer. You couldn't even tell for sure he'd been occupying the damp ground, since the rain was washing away all traces.

Jack reached over, touched a window pane of his studio. No blood stains left, all had been sluiced away.

"But he was dead," Jack said aloud. "There's no doubt about that."

That was sort of odd, too. Why had a rundown comic-book artist whom Jack hadn't laid eyes on for— hell, five years anyway—why'd he come to Brimstone, Connecticut to die in Jack's overgrown yard?

Moving his soaked, slippered feet with some effort, Jack started to work his way toward his front door.

That took him quite awhile.

Years ago he'd seen an old silent slapstick comedy— on some PBS documentary probably—in which the comedian had padded his legs with sponges for some reason or other and then walked into a series of lawn sprinklers. Jack felt like that now.

The door was half-open, just as it had been when he'd gone rushing out to find out what was wrong with Mutt.

"Well, I did find out. The poor bastard was dying."

He tripped over his own welcome mat, entered his hallway in a kneeling position.

After the spasm of pain had passed through him, Jack struggled to his feet.

He shrugged out of his water-soaked raincoat, staggered to the closet, and pulled the door open.

And he fell in love.

There was a very pretty young woman standing in the closet. Blond, tanned and a bit freckled, tall, about twenty-eight.

"You must be Sally," he said automatically.

"As a matter of fact, yes, I am." She was wearing a thick gray ski sweater and faded jeans and as she talked she rubbed the palm of her left hand along her thigh. "You'll really have to forgive me for hiding in your closet like this, except, and I guess it is sort of dippy of me, I got sort of scared. I heard gunshots a few minutes ago. The front door was open and I dived in here and hid. Force of habit in a way, I suppose."

"You've hidden in my closet before, you mean?"

"Not exactly, no. But, actually, we shouldn't be talking about me. You don't look very good, sort of like you got conked on the head and then fell over in the mud."

"I'm fairly sure that's about what did happen," he said. "Do you know Mutt Shermer?"

"Mutt?" She hesitated, then gave a negative shake of her head and stepped free of the closet. "No, I'm afraid not. Sort of an interesting name. Is he one of those high-society types, they all seem to have dippy names like—"

"Mutt was a second-rate comic-book artist. Somebody just killed him."

She inhaled sharply. "You're certain?"

"I saw him die."

She asked, "Where's his body?"

"Well, that's a problem of sorts." He bent, tugged off one of his soggy slippers and dropped it on the hardwood floor. "He was right outside my studio window, dead. But I got hit on the head. When I awakened, he was gone."

"Maybe Mutt isn't dead at all. This all could be a prank."

"People don't burn themselves with lighted cigarettes for a prank. Nope, Mutt is dead and gone and . . . I better phone the cops."

She touched his wet arm, frowning. "Why?"

"To report the murder of Mutt Shermer."

"I suppose, yes, you could consider that your civic duty and all," said Sally. "There is the danger, at least judging from what I've seen in movies and TV—I mean, I don't have any actual experience with vanishing corpses, but I suppose you could guess that just looking at me—although some of my friends swear I'm nowhere near as naive and guileless as I look—anyway, the police usually just laugh and deride people who claim to have seen a dead body. That is, if the body's no longer where it was supposed to be. They put their fingertips up beside their temples like this and rotate them. They might put restraints on you and, you know, haul you off to the psycho ward."

"Brimstone isn't a big enough town to have a psycho ward."

"They'll probably ship you over to the Norwalk Hospital. Especially since you're an artist. They'll naturally assume you were having a crazed drug orgy and started hallucinating about—"

"How do you know I'm an artist?"

"You mentioned a studio. I assumed that means you're an artist. Although you could just as well be a photographer, I suppose, or even a classical guitarist, since I read once that Segovia had a studio to practice—"

"Look, wait right here, okay? I'll go into my studio

9

and phone," he told her. "Or you can go sit in the living room."

"Is that the living room over yonder, with all the the packing crates strewn around?"

"I only recently moved in, everything isn't unpacked."

"How recently?"

"Well, five weeks. I'll be right back." He patted her arm, turned, and took a few sloshing steps along the hall. "Do you live around here, by the way?"

"Not exactly." She smiled tentatively.

He took one more look at her and walked around the bend in the hallway and into his studio.

Explaining everything to the Brimstone Police Department took just under ten minutes.

When he returned to the hallway, the pretty blonde was not there. She wasn't in the living room.

She wasn't—he opened it again to make sure—back in the closet.

The front door of his cottage was now shut.

"I wonder what's become of Sally," he murmured, touching at the sore spot on his head.

Chapter

2

At a few minutes after six the next morning Jack parked his disreputable VW bug in the rutted parking lot alongside Fagin's Diner on the Post Road in Westport. The rain had ceased during the night and the spring morning was clear and pale blue.

Jack bumped his sore head while extricating himself from the old car, winced, muttered a nondenominational curse, and walked over to the long, narrow brick restaurant.

Fagin himself, a grim, faded little man of fifty-four, was stationed behind the counter. He scowled at Jack, turned away and said something offensive to the nearest waitress.

"I love the clublike atmosphere of this place," Jack mentioned as he slid into the last booth.

Lew Goldberg, who was lean, dark, and thirty-one,

had the comic page of the *Brimstone Pilot* open next to his untouched plate of hotcakes. "Another gag about cockroaches in *Freddie Foible* today," he observed.

"Mine," admitted Jack.

"You don't seem to be bursting with health this morn. Didn't your jog over hill and dale at dawn infuse—"

"Didn't run."

Goldberg leaned back to scan his friend's face. "You ailing?"

"Got hit on the head last night."

"So you're dating again. I think that's a darn good idea," Goldberg said. "After all, your erstwhile wife fled the country over five months ago—"

"I got conked by persons unknown."

Resting his chin on his fist, Goldberg inquired, "How'd that happen? Myself, I've often been the victim of unsolicited assaults, but that's because of a personality some folks describe as a mite abrasive. You, however, are a gentle schlepp who—"

"You knew Mutt Shermer, didn't you?"

Goldberg puckered his cheek. "Don't tell me you're hanging around with him? The guy's a hoodoo." He folded up the newspaper, stowed it under his backside. "A crook, too, I heard tell. It was my impression he was serving time out West, on some sort of burglary charge. Never was much of an artist, though he kept coming up to the Maximus offices in Manhattan every now and then begging for work."

"He's dead."

Goldberg gave a shrug. "Don't think I'm going to act contrite about not speaking well of the dead," he said. "Mutt was a goniff and a disgrace to the profession. And being a disgrace to the profession of comic-book artist takes some doing. Does his passing have something to do with your getting conked?"

12

"Seems to. He died on my patio last night. When I was bending over him, I got hit."

"Classic situation. I've drawn it dozens of times, especially back when Maximus was publishing *Bloody Crimes Comics.* Never bend over a corpse, is a good rule to follow."

"I'll probably adopt that as policy from now on."

"Why'd Mutt pick your grounds to cash in his chips?"

"I don't know."

"He didn't explain?"

Jack turned, caught the eye of the redheaded waitress and made a pouring-a-cup-of-coffee gesture.

Smiling, she reached for the coffeepot.

Fagin glowered. "You a deaf mute all of a sudden, Deacon?"

"Eh, what say?" Jack cupped his hand to his ear.

"Artistes," sneered the grim proprietor.

Goldberg said, "So tell me the whole story about Mutt, rest his soul."

"He wasn't quite dead when I found him, or rather when he found me."

Goldberg snapped his fingers. "Hey, did the guy actually have a chance to deliver a dying message?"

"I think probably he did," replied Jack, "but first he asked for Sally."

"Good, the woman angle."

"Then he mumbled something about an AC . . . no a DC faucet." Jack paused while the plump waitress poured him a cup of coffee.

"Irene," said Goldberg in a low voice, "bring me a jelly donut and spread some extra jelly all over it."

"Fagin'd kill me."

"That's okay, as long as he does it after I get my donut."

"You're impossible." She gave him a faint smile and departed.

Jack stirred imitation cream into his coffee. "Sometimes I wish we all hadn't picked this spot as our early-morning hangout."

"It's an invigorating way to start each day. Continue."

"I don't know, Lew, I get the impression—there's something hidden somewhere and Mutt knows the location. He was damn anxious to pass it on, but he got sidetracked being cute."

"Yep, that's how dying messages are. Nobody ever simply says, 'I buried the doubloons next to the sundial.'"

Jack tried the coffee, which was godawful as usual. "Mutt told me the key to everything was—the Tijuana Bible," he said. "Doesn't mean anything to me, but maybe it's something that's well known down in Mexico or . . . what's the matter?"

Goldberg had started laughing. "That's right, you've always worked on newspaper strips and never sullied yourself with comic books."

"So?"

"I fear Mutt may have just been reliving past glories as he cashed it in," Goldberg informed him. "I've worked on them myself, years back when I was in my scuffling mode. Although I don't list that credit in my bio. Mutt did a lot of them."

"What are we talking about?"

"Tijuana Bibles, amigo," he answered, grinning. "That's a trade term for pornographic funny books. You know, eight-pagers, the kind men like."

"Hell," said Jack. "It sounded a lot more exotic to me. I had visions of a family Bible, leatherbound, gold-leafed, with some mysterious inscription hidden in its vellum pages."

"Sorry."

"But Mutt repeated it," said Jack. "Insisted it was the key to everything. The Tijuana Bible."

14

"Well, mayhap Sally knows what it means."

"I didn't get a chance to ask her."

"Hum?"

Leaning forward, resting both elbows on the Formica tabletop, he said, "I met this—she made a hell of an impression on me—I met this very pretty blonde and—"

"Skinny, right?"

"Slender, not built along the lines of a country-and-western singer, no. Not your type at all. Anyway, after I came to she was in my closet and—"

"Is this where the spooky music comes up and under, and I gaze at you as though I think you're goofy but don't want to mention it for fear you'll reach for the nearest chainsaw?"

"She was really there."

"In the closet?"

"Hiding."

"Folks do that often in your part of town, drop in for a little freelance hide-and-seek? 'Pardon us, Mr. Deacon, we all dropped in to hunker down in your mud room.' Amazing. All I get is housebreakers and an occasional irate husband."

"There was shooting. She ran into my place to hide."

"What was she doing in the neighborhood?"

"Just passing by, I imagine. I really—"

"You imagine? Didn't she get around to explaining?"

"She left."

"How?"

"When I was in my studio phoning the police."

Goldberg eyed him. "What do the cops think about her popping in and out in such a provocative fashion?"

"Actually I didn't mention her to them."

"Ah, I thought I read more than your usual straight-arrow gullibility in your face. You're smitten with the

15

underfed lass and you think you'll protect her from the—"

"Listen, they were having enough trouble believing me about Mutt Shermer. I didn't want to add a mystery woman."

"When you showed them the bloody corpse, didn't that go a long way toward banishing their—"

"The body was gone when I woke up from being slugged, Lew."

Goldberg shook his head, gazed briefly at the low, speckled ceiling of the diner. "And to think that all I did last night was ink three overdue pages of *Death Squad Two* for the great Maximus Comics empire. Why, I could have been over on your side of town having the time of my—"

"The cops poked around, even looked in that old carriage house. They couldn't find a trace of anything unusual. They debated about giving me a breath test or taking a urine sample. Then they left, saying they'd keep in touch."

Picking up his fork, Goldberg very carefully and thoughtfully cut the topmost pancake into neat quarters. "Rewind a bit and tell me the part about the faucet. Give me exactly what friend Mutt said to you."

Pressing his fingertips to his forehead, Jack thought about it for several silent seconds. "Something about a timely . . . that's right, a timely AC . . . no, DC faucet. And that somebody still had them all . . . or had had them all."

"Sure." Goldberg sat up, slapping at his knee. "Comic books, comic books."

"What?"

" 'Timely' is what the Marvel Comics folks used to call themselves back in the forties and fifties. DC is still one of the giants in the comic-book business, nearly as massive as my beloved Maximus. Fawcett, my boy, was one

16

of the other big ones back in what mouth-breathing fans dub the Golden Age. That's F-A-W-C-E-T-T. Not the plumbing faucet, but the Farah type."

"Why would Mutt tell me about old comic-book companies as he lay dying?"

"Why, for that matter, would he be eager to impart details about the porn business?" Goldberg scratched at his curly dark hair. "Could be he was simply incoherent at the end, but—what killed him anyway?"

"I'm not certain. I'd heard a shot before he came staggering up to my studio window," said Jack. "But I never had the chance to look him over. He'd been tortured, I'm near sure. Somebody'd burned his hands and face with cigarettes. Maybe his heart just gave out, maybe he was shot. With no corpse there's no way of knowing for sure."

"Torture," muttered Goldberg. "That means somebody wanted Mutt to talk about something."

"But it couldn't be about comic books."

"Nope, that doesn't make sense . . . unless . . ."

"Unless what?"

Goldberg's perpetual frown deepened. "Not sure. I had a vague hotflash about something. Mutt and old comic books. Lost it." He drummed his fingers on the Formica. "That would be an odd and strange treasure, though."

"Old comic books wouldn't be worth that much, would they?"

"Depends on which ones you have in your possession. There are some that, strange as it seems, are worth thousands of bucks. Sure. *Superman* number one, *Action* number one, *Marvel* number one, and so on. I saw a guy at a comics convention in Manhattan once who was displaying a collection of that sort of stuff and he maintained it was worth over a million dollars. Granted, your average drug dealer makes that in a day or so, but it ain't bad to peons such as we."

"Shit, we ought to be selling them instead of drawing them."

Lew cut each of the hotcake quarters neatly in half. "Are the police through with you?"

"Unless Mutt's body turns up someplace."

"Right now you know more than they do, though. You know for certain that there's somebody around who's killing people."

"I do, yes," agreed Jack.

"Furthermore, that somebody probably knows that you had a nice cozy chat with Mutt before he shuffled off this mortal coil."

"I don't think so. They didn't hit me until after he was dead," said Jack, making another try at his cup of coffee. "If they thought I knew something, they'd have tried to question me or dragged me off to wherever they took Mutt's remains."

"Maybe," said Goldberg, not convinced. "Or mayhap they know that you're a softhearted and currently horny fellow who'd go gaga over a skinny—excuse me—over a slim blonde pretending to be a damsel in distress. I bet she was the kind, this Sally, who batted her eyelashes and blushed a lot, correct?"

"No, she was a very straightforward, very intelligent woman. She did tend to babble a bit, but that was just because she was upset and—"

"See, I'm exactly right about this. You fell for the bait."

"Lew, you're forgetting that she's Sally. She's the one Mutt wanted to talk to, not the one who was involved in trying to torture him into talking."

"How do you know that, old chum?"

"She told me."

18

"That's not exactly the sort of proof that'd hold up in a court of law."

"She just happened to be in—"

"Just happened to be in your closet, were you going to say? C'mon, that doesn't make any sense at all," said Goldberg, thrusting the tines of his fork into a section of hotcake. "Okay, let's look at this from another angle. She is Sally, let's say, *the* Sally. Why the hell was she anywhere near *your* cottage last night? Why, for that matter, was Mutt there? What it sounds like is that there was supposed to be a rendezvous, between Mutt and this willowy blonde. Now then, how'd the killers know about the get-together? Most folks are of the opinion that Mutt's still basking in the slammer out in California."

Jack let out his breath. "If I could answer those questions I'd be a hell of a lot further along than I am."

"Further along toward what—getting your own pass to the hereafter?"

"I'd like to find," he said, "—Sally."

"Remember what happened to Gatsby when he went chasing after Daisy? Same thing or worse is likely to—"

"She's probably in trouble."

"Okay, look her up in the phone book and call her, inquire if she's in . . . you're grimacing and, since you haven't tasted the food yet, it must be something else."

"I don't know her last name."

"Great. Seems to me if I found a woman in my closet, the first thing I'd get was name, address, and serial number."

"I had a lot on my mind."

"My opinion, and I've had a great deal of experience with troublesome ladies, is that this Sally is guaranteed bad news. People with guns are found in her vicinity. People with guns who like to snuff their cigarettes out

19

on human flesh just to hear the sizzle." He held up a cautionary finger. "Forget her."

Jack shook his head. "Don't think I can."

Fagin called out, "Hey, Deacon, if you want to get your breakfast at the special price, you got exactly fifty-two seconds left to get your order in."

Chapter

3

Mutt Shermer had died and vanished on Tuesday night. The manila envelope arrived in Thursday's mail.

Jack had pushed back from his drawing board a few minutes after one in the afternoon, having finished inking a *Freddie Foible* Sunday page. He wandered into his tiny kitchen, described by his real-estate lady as snug, and fixed himself a tuna-salad sandwich in a pita-bread pocket. The pita had a few bluish blotches on it that might be mold and Jack made a note on the memo pad magnetically affixed to the small refrigerator—"Buy bread."

The spring afternoon was warm, clear. He carried the sandwich and a can of iced tea out onto the snug patio. Before settling into the lone deck chair, abandoned there by a previous tenant, he deposited the sandwich plate and the can of tea on the striped canvas of the chair and went out to the road to check his mailbox.

A couple weeks back some marauding teenage louts had attacked all the mailboxes along this winding lane. Jack's was now dented, speckled with rust and leaning far to the left on its wooden post.

"Got to fix this darn thing," he said aloud as he extracted his mail. He stood there going through it.

Two bills, an ad from a firm that steam-cleaned carpets, an ad from a bank that would loan him $50,000 if he but met certain simple standards, a bright picture postcard from Brazil—no message on it, but he knew it was from his wife, who still apparently got a kick out of taunting him now and then—and a nine- by twelve-inch manila envelope. It had no return address, had been postmarked in nearby Norwalk, and was addressed to Sally Westerland, 104 Witch Hill Lane, Brimstone, Connecticut 06883.

"Of course," he said.

The address was his, but the name must be that of the blond young woman who'd visited his closet the other night.

"Sure, that explains it. She used to live here at one time. Mutt thought she still did and he came here to talk to her."

Jack started back for the cottage.

"Okay, but how'd she know he was going to come here?"

Maybe she told him to meet her here.

"Nope, that doesn't figure. You wouldn't arrange a secret meeting at somebody else's place."

Wait now, go back. Mutt is probably the one who mailed this envelope to Sally—to Sally Westerland. That means he was still using her old address and phone number. He calls her on the phone, she an-

swers, he tells her he's coming over to see her on
urgent business.

Jack found himself inside his small living room.

He tossed everything but the envelope atop a cardboard carton, sat in his imitation Morris chair.

"If Sally's still living in Brimstone, then she probably kept the same phone number she had when she lived here. Sure, the phone company always does that when you move from one part of the same town to another. So Mutt phones her, says, 'I'm heading right over to pass on important information about lost treasure.' He hangs up before they do much talking. It's only when he's late that Sally starts suspecting that he may've come to her old address."

Right, because Mutt, according to Goldberg, has been in the pokey out in California somewhere. The last time he visited Sally she was right here on Witch Hill Lane.

Jack tapped the envelope on his knee.

"But somebody else caught up with Mutt and killed him."

How the hell did the killer know Mutt was coming here?

"Tailed him or . . ."

Or Sally sent the killer.

"No, she wouldn't do that and then show up on the scene herself."

She didn't expect to be discovered here, though. It was only by chance that you spotted her.

"She's not a killer, or a girl who hires killers."

But she's a liar.

"How so?"

She swore to you she didn't know Mutt Shermer.

"Maybe she doesn't."

C'mon, you just worked out the whole chain, prov-

23

ing that he came here expecting to find her and that he'd phoned her first.

"True, but . . ."

Of course, if this envelope isn't from Mutt—if it contains maybe a seed catalog or a sweepstakes entry blank—then she probably isn't involved in this at all.

"No way of finding that out unless I open the damn thing."

Wouldn't be that hard. No tape on the flap. Just undo the clasp and steam the glue a little.

He took a few short breaths, mouth open.

Jack stood, tucked the envelope under his arm, and went into his studio.

He grabbed the phone, dialed Goldberg's number.

"Hello, this is not a recording but the honest and true Lew Goldberg."

"It's Jack. You busy?"

"Just about to start penciling a nineteen-page *Kalifornia Killbillies* story. Thus I'm eager for any excuse to postpone the chore."

"Could you maybe come over, Lew? I think I'm facing a moral dilemma."

"Those are the best kind," said Goldberg. "I'll be right over."

———

Goldberg leaned forward on the packing carton. "Well?"

"Yep, she's listed here in the Brimstone section of the phone book," answered Jack, who had the directory opened across his lap. "Sally Westerland, twenty-six Poverty Hollow Road."

"That'd be an apt address for me," observed the curly haired cartoonist. "All right, that seems to confirm part of your theory. The elusive Sally does live in

24

Brimstone still and quite probably has the same phone number now as she enjoyed while residing here."

"Meaning Mutt, who'd been away, could've called the number and gotten through to her, not realizing she had a new address."

"Seems likely." He popped to his feet, commenced pacing. "One thing bothers me."

"Which?"

"Why would a lady attractive enough to drive you mad with passion be making a date with a schlub like Mutt Shermer?"

Jack said, "My impression is he was trying to deliver a message from somebody else. You know, he said something about 'he still had them.'"

Stopping his pacing among the unpacked moving boxes, Goldberg pointed at the manila envelope on the coffee table. "Suppose the Tijuana Bible is in there?"

"That occurred to me."

"We've been assuming that Mutt was alluding to a cache of valuable comic books, but perhaps he was really talking about narcotics or stolen government secrets."

"Naw, I don't really—"

"Seems to me, old buddy, that it's our duty as loyal citizens to take a look inside that telltale envelope."

"Yeah, I'd like to, but—"

"Consider this, Jack. A man was slaughtered on your patio, a strange woman used your closet as a hideout, the police doubt your sanity— Have you heard from them again, by the way?"

"No, and there hasn't been anything in the papers about finding a body remotely resembling Mutt's."

"Very well, then. We have here yet another classic situation. Innocent young man must take desperate steps to clear his good name."

25

"Thirty-seven isn't exactly young."

"Close enough. Give me the envelope, please." He held out his hand, fingers beckoning.

Jack hesitated a few seconds, then passed it over. "If that's just a personal letter from a—"

"Anybody close to the lady'd know her current whereabouts—unless he'd been locked away in the clink." Goldberg seated himself in a canvas chair, examined the flap of the envelope. "Ah, a cinch for Jimmy Valentine. I won't even have to sandpaper my fingertips."

"Maybe I ought to phone her before we—"

"Don't natter while I'm at work." He pried the clasp open, worked his little finger under the flap. "Cheap glue, doesn't hold very well. Ouch, damn it, a paper cut."

The flap came free. Goldberg upended the envelope and shook its contents out onto the coffee-table top.

"It is," said Jack.

A thin comic book, about six by eight inches, had landed on the table. It was entitled *Superdork* and had an appropriate drawing on its black and red cover.

"My first impulse is to hold this at arm's length," said Goldberg, picking up the pornographic comic book and scanning the cover. "It's unsigned, obviously, but I'm pretty certain Mutt Shermer drew this."

"I don't know his style."

"It's Mutt's lack of style that helps you identify his efforts." Goldberg, gingerly, turned through the pages of the Tijuana Bible. "Interesting story line. Superdork has his way with Blunder Woman, Rat Girl, and Betty Boobs, et cetera. Hey, wait. Here he's teamed up with the Prone Ranger, in more ways than one. Take a gander at this next page."

Almost the entire page of the two-color comic book

was taken up by a map. "The Lost Poontang Mine," read Jack. "Mutt wasn't much of a letterer either."

"You're missing the point, chum. This isn't really a map of Pike's Prick and environs as it states, it's really California."

"Yeah, so it is. And somebody put three X's in blue on three of these fictitious spots."

Goldberg said, "This map has to be what Mutt wanted Sally to have."

"We still don't know why."

"That's one of the things you're going to have to ask her."

Chapter

4

He arrived there, alone and unannounced, at a few minutes beyond eight that evening.

The house on Poverty Hill Road was a small saltbox, about twice the size of the cottage Jack was now occupying. Light showed at two of the draped downstairs windows.

Jack had parked in a cul-de-sac downhill and come walking back up to Sally Westerland's house. Off in the wooded acres across the dark road a dog barked twice and then quit.

Jack shifted the manila envelope to his left hand as he climbed the red-brick front steps.

He took a deep breath before pushing the bell button.

That produced no audible sound within.

He tried again.

Still no evidence the bell was functioning.

Taking hold of the gargoyle knocker, he whacked it a few times.

After about a minute he thought he heard the sound of soft footfalls.

"Why didn't you just walk in instead of making all this darn . . . Oh, I thought you were someone else." Sally, wearing a short yellow terry robe, had yanked the front door open.

"Apparently." He attempted a smile. "I'm Jack Deacon. I don't know if you remember, but we met a couple nights ago when you were hiding in my closet."

She smiled a little uneasily. "Yes, I haven't forgotten," she said, eyeing him. "How'd you locate me?"

He held up the envelope. "There's an interesting story that goes with it," he told her. "Maybe if I could come in and explain what exactly—"

"I suppose you could. I'm getting ready to go out, but maybe it won't take long."

"No way of telling."

"Come on in anyway. Jack, is it?"

"Jack Deacon. I'm a cartoonist." He followed her along a gray-carpeted hallway and into a stark white, yellow, and black living room. "Maybe you don't know about the social habits of cartoonists, but most of them know each other. Don't necessarily like each other in all cases, but know each other. That's how I know Mutt Shermer."

"My father was an illustrator. That's not all that far from a cartoonist."

He said, "Hubert Westerland. Magazine illustrator, one of the founders of the Westport Artists School. I should've connected the—"

"You had something to tell me?"

Jack was sniffing the air. "Cinammon," he said.

"I'm baking rice pudding, and trying to get ready for a date."

"The damn sandwich," said Jack, mostly to himself.

"Beg pardon?"

"Nothing, I just now remembered I left my lunch out on the patio this afternoon." He walked over to the deep, empty blackstone fireplace. "As you know, Miss Westerland, I live in the house you used to live in."

"I didn't know that, no."

"Sure, you did. You saw me in it Tuesday night."

"Which doesn't prove I ever lived there."

"Well, I went and looked it up in some old phone directories at the Brimstone Library and you did—for two years up until last year." He held up the envelope again. "Mutt Shermer mailed this to you at that old address. He's been out of circulation and thought you were still on Witch Hill."

The pretty blond young woman shook her head. "I'm really afraid you aren't conveying much to me, Mr. . . . Dinkins, was it?"

"Deacon," he supplied. "What do you do for a living?"

"I'm an actress," she answered. "At least I was. Shortly after my father died last year I started looking after what's left of the W.A.S. operation. Although, frankly, Mr. Deacon, I don't see that any of this concerns you in the least."

"Tuesday night you were playing a different type," he said, grinning. "Lovable scatterbrain, a sort of younger Goldie Hawn. Tonight it's more Grace Kelly dealing with the peasantry." He sat down, uninvited, in a large black armchair and propped the manila envelope on one knee. "Okay, you're a very attractive girl and a terrific actress, judging from the samples I've seen. The thing is, somebody killed Mutt Shermer Tuesday night. He was very anxious to get a message to you and I think he also wanted you to have whatever is in this envelope. I came up here expecting to run into that wide-eyed innocent young woman I met two nights ago. Shows that I'm still a rube at heart." He paused, watching her face. "Either you explain to me something about what the hell is going on or I turn this over to the cops *and* I give them an account of what Mutt said before he died."

"You haven't done that as yet?"

"I didn't think it would help my case much, since they already had me down as somebody who was probably demented."

Sally twisted the belt of the lemon-yellow robe around her forefinger. "This all sounds very interesting—no it sounds entertaining," she said. "However, I simply don't know any Mutt Shermer and I'm not expecting a present from him."

He nodded, his tongue poking his cheek out. "And it was just a coincidence that you happened to be in the vicinity of my cottage?"

"I like to take walks at night."

"You're four and a half miles across town from me."

"Long walks." She gestured at the manila envelope. "Is that addressed to me, by the way?"

"It is, yep."

"Then you'd best hand it over before you go. Actually, you know, it's a federal crime to tamper with or impede the mail."

"Look, why not be a shade more open with—"

"Sal?" The sound of the front door banging open came rolling down the hall and into the room.

"In here, Buzz."

Heavy footsteps, followed by a large wide man of about thirty-five. Red-faced, crew-cut, in a tight gray business suit. He scowled at Jack, asked the young woman, "Who's the putz?"

31

"Buzz, please now," said Sally. "This is Jack Deacon. Buzz Wisebecker."

"What's this putz doing here?"

"Mr. Deacon just dropped over to deliver a package. He's on his way—"

"A package, huh?" The big florid man took a few steps in Jack's direction. "Is it the stuff from Shermer, Sal? Is that what that old fart did with it?"

"Well, it may be, Buzz. We can certainly discuss that after—"

"It's the goddamn Tijuana Bible, isn't it?"

"I haven't opened the envelope yet, but I imagine it might well—"

"That's just fine. Hey, that's just really fine." Wisebecker's beefy right hand rushed inside his jacket and snapped out, clutching a .38 revolver. "On your feet, putz."

"Hold it now," suggested Jack, starting to rise. "There's no reason to—"

"Sally, move around over there next to him."

The young woman blinked, shook her head slowly. "What the heck are you—"

"Go on, go on. I want the both of you together." He gestured at her, using the gun. "Move it, come on."

"Buzz, whenever you have a few drinks after—"

"Move, now! Stand next to the putz."

Jack said, "Possibly you're a mite ticked off because you walked in to find your girlfriend with a stranger and wearing only a skimpy robe. I can assure you that we—"

"Now, putz, you hand me that envelope. Very slowly and politely, okay?" He made a come-closer motion with the revolver. "That's fine. Stretch out your arm and pass it over. Good, good." Wisebecker snatched the envelope with his free hand, opened it one-handed and sneaked a quick glance inside. "Yeah, it's the Tijuana Bible for sure."

Sally, who was standing near Jack and hugging herself, said, "You've been conning me, Buzz. These past months. All you were interested in was—"

"You got it," he agreed, chuckling. "Now I want the both of you to head for the basement. Sal, you'll tie the putz up and then I'll truss you. After which, I'll depart."

As they were being herded toward the basement stairway, Sally leaned close to Jack and said, "I haven't been exactly truthful with you."

"I suspected as much," he said.

Chapter

5

Sally said, "There aren't any rats in my basement."

Jack said, "One just crawled over me."

"Probably a mouse."

"It weighed about five pounds."

"A healthy mouse."

"Felt like a rat."

"Are you used to having rodents crawl over you, so that you can distinguish—"

"Nope, as a matter of fact, this is the first time I've ever been trussed up hand and foot and dumped on the hard concrete floor of a damp, moldering cellar."

"It isn't damp and moldering. I've got a practically new dehumidifier down here that—"

"Maybe in that chair your paramour tied you to it's dry and cozy, but down here on the floor it's, I guarantee you, damp and moldering. Not to mention rat-infested."

Sally said, "Don't blame me because Buzz took the trouble to tie me to this old straightback chair instead of dumping me down there on the floor. He's apparently—despite the fact he's turned out to be a sneaky son of a bitch—he's apparently got a thoughtful side."

"Exactly. He didn't want you sprawled on this chill stone floor and the prey of plague-ridden rats."

"C'mon, Mr. Deacon, there hasn't been a case of plague in this part of Connecticut for years."

"Look, since we're probably going to rot away together down here—you may as well call me Jack."

"We'll get out."

"How?"

She said, "I'm assuming you'll think of something."

"Your nearest neighbor is about a quarter mile downhill, so yelling isn't—"

"They're vacationing in Switzerland anyway."

"Even farther away." Jack rocked his shoulders from side to side and worked his knees up and down. Gradually he dragged himself a few inches closer to the blond young woman.

He'd been left facedown, hands tied behind his back with green plastic clothesline and ankles tightly bound with the same stuff, on a patch of cleared basement floor between stacks of string-tied magazines and a pile of large cardboard cartons labeled *Property Westport Artists School.*

Sally, her terry robe twisted awkwardly, was in a sturdy wooden chair and tied thoroughly to it with more of the green line. The chair was backed up against floor-to-ceiling raw wood shelves. The shelves held stacked paperback books, assorted shoeboxes,

35

and, high up, a row of jars that might contain preserved cherries.

There was one light, a naked sixty-watt bulb dangling from a frayed black cord over near the oil furnace.

"I suppose," said Sally, watching him wriggle his way nearer to her, "I owe you an apology. After all, you meant well when you came barging into—"

"What you owe me, Sally, is a goddamn explanation."

She didn't immediately reply. "I don't really know if that's necessary," she said finally.

"I think it is. I'd like to die relatively content, which I can't do if I don't know why I've been tied up and dropped down a rathole."

"Are you always this pessimistic, Jack?"

He snaked another foot over the cold gray floor, his groin passing over some sort of small garden tool he hadn't noticed before. "Yep, every time a madman leaves me to die, I foolishly let it get me down."

"Buzz isn't exactly insane. He's just incredibly—and I should've noticed that before—mercenary."

"This is about money?" The garden tool—it felt like one of those things you claw weeds with—was now making its way along his left leg.

"Well, something that's worth a good deal of money."

"Jesus, it *is* comic books, isn't it? Goldberg was right."

"Who's Goldberg?"

"Lew Goldberg, a friend of mine. The point is, there's some kind of cache of old comic books hidden someplace, isn't there?"

"Well, yes."

"And we're both going to rot away in a cellar over funny books."

"A million and a half dollars worth," she said slowly.

36

"That's what Buzz was really interested in, while I, more fool, thought he was fond of—"

"Quit that," he advised as he continued to slither closer to her. "What the hell's the matter with you? You're a terrific-looking woman, bright and intelligent and talented. Why fret over an oaf like Buzz Wisebecker?"

"You're right I suppose," Sally admitted, watching his slow progress. "It's only that I tend to keep getting involved with the same kind of loutish man."

"Do they all tie you up when they depart?"

"No, Buzz is the first."

Jack paused to take a few deep breaths. "I haven't been all that lucky of late myself," he admitted. "Even before I ran into you I wasn't doing that well. For example, my wife recently ran off—"

"To South America with an admiral or something," said Sally. "Took all your money and left you cold."

"How'd you know that?"

"I think I heard some cartoonists talking about you in Gold's deli in Westport a few weeks back. Yes, Jack Deacon. They were all laughing." She shook her head. "But from the way they were describing you, I thought you'd be . . . um."

"Be what?" He commenced crawling again.

"I guess more of a schmuck."

Jack said, "Here I am trussed up like a sacrificial goat, crawling on my belly across your basement—doesn't that qualify me as a schmuck?"

"But you're doing that so we can get together and work out a means of escape, aren't you?"

"Actually I want to get closer to the furnace. It's freezing over where Buzz tossed me."

"Now you're trying to downplay yourself. See, men like Buzz never do that. They're continually doing their

37

own PR, making everything they do seem even better than it is," she said. "You, on the other hand, tend to mask your accomplishments. Unfortunately, I usually end up with the ones like Buzz."

"Suppose," he requested, pausing about five feet from her chair, "you explain who Buzz is exactly."

Sally said, "You know about my father—he and Jarrett Cobb founded the Westport Artists School something like thirty years ago."

"I know, I even signed up for one of the W.A.S. mail-order courses when I was a kid."

"Yes, the school has taught a lot of now-successful artists to—"

"But not me. When I fell behind in my payments, they made me send the lessons back."

"Most of our students around the country paid," continued the young woman. "My father and Cobb became quite wealthy, within five years of founding the school. But about six years ago, at the urging of Cobb, W.A.S. started to diversify. Into audio and video teaching, into book and magazine publishing. We began to lose money, quite a lot of money. After my father died I became Cobb's partner."

"He's not much of an illustrator."

"Cobb's not much of a human being," she said. "Two years ago he suggested we hire Buzz to handle our advertising and public relations. He'd been with a good PR firm in Manhattan, with an ad agency out in San Francisco before that. Initially, at least, Buzz did help us increase our mail enrollments." She paused, sighing softly. "About three months ago I suddenly became convinced he was attractive and started dating him. Another triumph of Buzz's selling ability, I guess."

"What had you thought of him before that?"

"Not much. He was still doing a fair job for W.A.S., though we weren't exactly forging ahead. What we've been doing lately is just sinking into oblivion a bit more slowly than before."

"You trusted Buzz?"

Sally nodded ruefully. "I shouldn't have, but I did."

He was nearer her chair, only a foot or so away. "Okay, now tell me about the comic books."

"How much do you know about the value of old comics?"

"Some. Goldberg works for Maximus and he's filled me in about how much some of the rarer ones from the thirties and forties can be worth."

"All right," she said. "For the last fifteen years before he died, my father collected what they call Golden Age comic books. Those published from roughly between 1935 and, say, 1950. Then comes the Silver Age, which he wasn't especially interested in."

"He collected them as an investment or because he liked the things?"

"Both. He actually had worked in the comic-book field, for a short time, just after the Second World War. So it was partly nostalgia, too."

"And his collection is worth a million and a half dollars?"

"At least. I have the list up in my den, I'll show it to you."

"Eventually." Jack finally reached her.

"You're sounding a bit more optimistic."

"I don't suppose you can do anything with your toes?"

"Such as?"

"Untie my hands. Since you're barefoot, I thought maybe—"

"I think you need a chimpanzee for that sort of work, Jack."

"Okay, it was just a rough notion. That's how I do

39

gags for *Freddie Foible*—just babble suggestions until something workable comes out."

"That's right, you're an assistant on the strip."

"Were they talking about that at Gold's, too?"

"Wally Warfield was a good friend of my father's and I still run into him now and then."

"Tools. That thing I crawled over. Are there any tools stored down here, something we can use to slice through these lines?"

"There's a tool cabinet next to the furnace."

"Good, maybe I can crawl over and—"

"It's locked, Jack."

"Locked?"

"My father taught me to take care of valuable possessions."

"Where's the key?"

"In a drawer of my desk upstairs."

"What was that I bumped into on the floor back there?"

"A weeder, but it's not sharp enough to cut through plastic."

"Knives?"

"Up in the kitchen."

"Cherries."

"How can cherries do any—"

"Didn't I see some jars of cherries up on these shelves?"

"Well, yes. My late mother canned them and I've been lugging them around from rental to rental as a sort of sentimental—"

"Glass." He rocked from side to side. "If we can break any of the jars, we'll get some hunks of glass. Maybe we can cut through this stuff that way."

"I don't know. My mother wasn't all that domestic during her lifetime and these cherries are just about the only memento I have of that aspect of her—"

40

"When did she put them up?"

Sally considered. "Oh, it's about fifteen years ago."

"How many jars have you eaten since then?"

"None. I don't much like cherries, especially those little pale pink puckered-up ones. Yet I—"

"I may not be able to do this anyway." He succeeded, after considerable thrashing about, in rolling over onto his back. After a few substantial grunts, he managed to get his legs raised up.

"Do you do much exercising?"

"Every day."

"From the way you're huffing and puffing, I'd rate you as a typical sedentary artist who—"

"I also run." He kicked out with his feet at the rickety shelving. "Occasionally."

"Darn."

A dozen fat paperback novels had come cascading down to land in Sally's lap.

"Do you read those steamy historical novels?" He kicked out again, then twice more.

More books fell, missing Sally and landing with a combined thump on his midsection.

"I went through a phase some years ago," she answered. "And somebody who draws a comic strip about cockroaches is in no position to criticize the taste of—"

"*Freddie Foible* isn't about cockroaches—cockroaches are simply one of its many motifs."

"All this week it's been nothing but cockroaches."

"Well, sometimes I go through a cockroach phase," he admitted, kicking the shelves again and causing his leg muscles considerable pain.

But this assault on the shelves brought down a jar of cherries. It came plummeting, along with three shoe boxes and a thesaurus.

"Jack, look out!"

41

He jerked aside and the jar smashed less than a foot from his head.

One of the shoe boxes, though, slammed into his chest. "Oof," he remarked, watching its contents come tumbling free. "A box of doorknobs?"

"My father taught me not to throw away something that might be useful someday," Sally explained. "Those cherries don't smell all that good, do they?"

"Godawful is, I think, the correct gastronomical term."

"Poor mom."

"When did she die?"

"Ten years ago."

"Any brothers or sisters?"

Sally didn't reply.

"Sally?" He was maneuvering around on the floor, trying to get his tied hands in the vicinity of the broken jar without slicing up any important sections of his body.

Sally said at last, "You don't know about my brother?"

"Nope, not a thing. Myself, I'm an only child."

"That's usually the best way to be."

"It's that bad, huh?"

She answered, "My brother is the one who stole all the comic books from my father."

Chapter

6

"Ouch," said Sally, wincing.

"Over the past few hours," said Jack, "we've gotten to know each other a bit better, Sal. But, please, don't yell *ouch* every time I cut myself."

"I empathize with you," she told him. "And I am, after all, supposed to be advising you, since I can see what you're doing and you can't. Something like a navigator."

Jack was sprawled on his stomach again in front of the chair she was tied in. He had a sharp fragment of jar, about the size of a monocle, gripped in the fingers of his right hand and he had been hacking at the green plastic line around his wrists for nearly fifteen painful minutes now.

"If you slice your hands all up, you won't be able to draw anymore."

"If I molder away on the floor of your basement, that'll screw up my artistic career even more."

"Ouch. Sorry."

"Tell me some more about your brother."

"Well, Shawn—spelled S-H-A-W-N, not the traditional S-E-A-N, and don't ask me why because I could never get my mother to explain. Shawn was a great brother—within the limits of how great any brother can be—until he reached the age of fifteen. He's two years younger than I am and—ouch. Sorry, excuse me. Then when Shawn reached fifteen, he just went to pieces. Trouble in school, first pranks and mischief, then cutting classes, flunking courses, petty thefts. It kept accelerating—drugs, housebreaking, stealing cars. We went through juvenile court, just missed criminal court later on. My father got Shawn to see a very good, and very expensive, therapist. That seemed to help and in his early twenties he was really quite nice again. But it didn't last. He got back into drugs, heavier stuff this time—coke mostly. And we were pretty sure he was starting to deal the stuff and was getting involved with other sorts of crime. Then about a year before my father died, Shawn just took off. Very late one evening he somehow got all the comic books—they were stored in three huge steamer trunks that were souvenirs of my father's art student days in Paris and Rome—Shawn loaded them into a ratty old van he had and just drove off. I haven't seen him since."

"He probably sold the comics years ago."

She said, "No, he never sold them, not according to Mutt Shermer."

"Mutt—how's he fit in?"

"You think he's dead, do you?"

"Not an opinion, Sal. Mutt died in my yard."

"That's my fault really."

"He was supposed to be meeting you."

44

"Yes, but I originally thought Mutt was coming here. By the time I realized he thought I still lived where you're living, it was too late."

"Who else knew about the meeting?"

"Nobody," she answered. "Wait—Buzz knew, of course. He was here when Mutt phoned the other night and he said he had to go right after the call." She shuddered, shaking her head. "But, Jack, that must mean Buzz is involved in the killing."

"Directly or indirectly, sure," he said. "Whoever killed Mutt questioned him first, tortured the guy."

"My fault again. He was loyal to my brother, and he wanted me to have the comic books."

"Where's your brother?"

Very quietly she began to cry. "Dead. According to Mutt, Shawn got into trouble with some drug dealers down in Mexico. This was about a year ago and he hid out from them for quite awhile, but then they caught up with him. He's dead."

"If you can believe somebody like Mutt."

"He died rather than tell them anything."

"That's one assumption."

"It has to be that way, otherwise Buzz wouldn't have waited around to grab that Tijuana Bible," she said. "If Mutt had told them where the comic books are stashed—even if he knew—Buzz would have been off searching long ago."

"Wait now. Didn't Mutt know?"

"Mutt told me on the phone he didn't, that he was bringing me the porno comic book with the map in it," she said. "Then when he called the other night he said he was sending the book by mail, because he was uneasy about losing it. But he wanted to see me anyway and tell me about my brother."

Jack was getting the notion he'd nearly succeeded in

sawing through a strand of cord. "Am I almost through one at least?"

"I wish I'd had time to put in my contacts before we—"

"You've been guiding me blind?"

"No, I can make out your fingers and wrists more or less. Yes, you have a piece of line almost cut. Move the glass a smidgen to a right and—"

"How much is a smidgen in inches?"

"About an eighth. There, you've got it. Now saw right at that spot."

The cord snapped. "Success at last." He tugged, trying to yank his wrists apart, but they remained tied.

"I think," she said, squinting down at him, "that if you work on the cord just below the other one, that'll maybe do it."

He commenced sawing. "How do you know the comics are still hidden someplace?"

"Mutt told me. You see, he phoned me first about a week ago, told me about my brother's death and that Shawn wanted me to have the comics—about the map and the Tijuana Bible," she replied.

"Where'd your brother hide them?"

"Mutt only knew they're in California—either all in one spot or maybe split up and stashed in three different places."

"Sure, that explains the three marks on the map."

"Marks on the map? Careful with that glass, you're getting close to a vein, I think. Are you implying you got a look at the map?"

"I took a peek at the Tijuana Bible," he admitted. He told her about having opened the envelope, with the help of Goldberg, and taking a look.

"I think that's called tampering with the mail. That package was addressed to me and—"

"Think of it this way, Sally. If I hadn't done it, we

wouldn't have any idea where that million-and-a-half dollars worth of comic books might be."

"You're saying you memorized the map?"

"Sure, I've got a pretty good graphic memory. If I don't cut off any more of my fingers, I'll draw you a copy once we're loose."

"Buzz has still got a head start."

"Yeah, but the map's in code. You should be able to figure it out ahead of him, since your brother—"

"Give me an example of the code."

"In a while." He gave a strong tug and the second strand separated. In less than a minute his hands were free and he was sitting up, flexing his fingers. "You're going to need help on this treasure hunt."

"I'm afraid I'm also going to need financing," she said. "Most of my money is tangled up in W.A.S. I think I have maybe enough credit left on one of my cards to arrange a one-way flight to California."

"I have an idea about how we can finance the trip." He started untying his ankles. "What we have to work out first is some kind of partnership deal."

"You and me?"

He nodded. "I've got some vacation time coming and this sounds interesting," he said. "And I guess I'd like to beat Buzz to the loot."

"You want a percentage of what we end up with, is that it?"

"How's fifty–fifty?"

"No, can't do that." She shook her head vehemently. "Twenty percent and no more. After all, they're my father's comic books—stolen by my own brother. It's a family matter really."

"Forty percent."

Sally sighed, indicating she was somewhat disappointed in him. "Thirty-five percent or forget it."

47

He stood up and kicked away the last of the clothes-line. "Okay, that's good enough. We have a deal."

"Could you please undo me now."

"Sure, I was just waiting," he said, smiling down at her, "until you agreed to the thirty-five."

Sally yawned once as she guided her crimson Porsche through the winding dawn lanes of Brimstone. She was wearing a white cablestitch sweater, a pair of faded designer jeans, and a pair of raggedy pale blue deck shoes. Her blond hair was pulled back and tied with a single twist of black ribbon. "We'd best check Buzz's place first."

"He's likely to be winging westward by now."

"Even so, a look around there might turn up a clue," she said. "About who he's in cahoots with and where he's heading first."

"You've got a key?"

She didn't answer, asking him, "Can you draw while we're moving?"

"Sure." Jack had a sketchbook he'd extracted from his VW resting in his lap.

"You don't get car-sick?"

"Nope."

"I even get butterflies if I read on the train."

"Probably those torrid historical romances that cause chronic stomach-churning."

"I haven't read one of those for years."

Nodding, Jack concentrated on reproducing the map he'd seen in the *Superdork* pornographic comic book. "Wouldn't it have been simpler for your brother to have just phoned you at some point and told you where he'd hidden the comic books and how to re-trieve them?"

"From what I gathered from my two fairly brief con-

48

versations with poor Mutt," she said, swinging the car around a curve, "Shawn had intended eventually to get them himself. He had Mutt draw that map originally for his own reference. His memory wasn't all that terrific after several years of attempting to fry it with drugs and sundries."

"And he only made one copy marked with the three X's?"

"Yes, that's the one he was carrying around—and then passed to Mutt, when he began to suspect he might never be able to come back."

The day was starting, the gray of the early morning was giving way to a thin, clear blue and the maples and pines lining the back road were brightening.

"Circumlocution," said Jack, chewing on the cap of his pen and frowning at the nearly finished map.

"But that's the way Shawn was. He liked games and intrigues, puzzles and tricks. He could be a pain in the butt sometimes, but I loved him—usually."

"Rumors I've heard indicated Mutt was locked away in prison someplace."

"Yes, he hinted at that. He told me that my brother had entrusted him with the task of getting the Tijuana Bible to me awhile ago," she said, sniffling. "Soon as Mutt got out of wherever he'd been cooped up, he went to where he'd hidden the porno comic, got it, and headed for Connecticut."

"Sounds like more loyalty than Mutt was capable of."

"Shawn brought out that sort of loyalty in people sometimes." She glanced over at what he was drawing. "You don't have a very good lettering style, for a professional cartoonist."

"For lettering done in a wildly careening sportscar this isn't all that bad, Sal."

"Finished?"

49

"Just about. I'm trying to remember a couple more things." He leaned back in the seat and closed his eyes.

"Don't take a nap."

"Of all the women I've ever spent the night with, you are one of the most critical the morning after."

"Don't go mistaking honest concern and anxiety for some sort of put-down of you. It isn't. And, by the way, although I didn't mention it last night, I really don't like to be called Sal."

"Noted." He opened his eyes, leaned forward, and, very carefully, lettered in two final place names on the re-creation of the map. "What your brother had Mutt draw as the alleged map of the Lost Poontang Mine is actually a map of roughly two thirds of the state of California, from about Lake Tahoe at the top to just below Long Beach at the bottom. There are assorted whimsical town names—Putzburg, Chicockso, et cetera."

Sally took a quick look, then returned her attention to the early-morning road. The houses thereabouts were all on two-acre lots rich with trees and greenery. "What are the names of the three towns you've checked?"

"Far as I can recall these are the same three your brother marked. One's north of San Francisco and is called Uncle John's Burg." He turned, watching her profile.

Sally said, "When we were kids, we went to California a lot, vacationed all over the state. Uncle John is an honorary uncle. His name is Giovanni Macri and he was a good friend of my father. In fact, dad designed some of the labels for Uncle John's winery."

"That'd be the Macri Brothers Winery?"

"That's the one, yes, located in Sonoma County in a little town named Clarinda."

"My wife and I used to like their chablis—in happier times."

50

Sally's nose wrinkled. "They produce an awful chablis," she told him. "The only halfway tolerable Macri Brothers wine is their rosé—and even that depends on the year."

"So Uncle John's Burg is Clarinda, California?"

"Got to be. Which means that part or all of the missing collection of comic books is at the winery somewhere."

"Would Uncle John keep stolen goods for your brother?"

"Nobody knew about Shawn's swiping them—and Uncle John didn't even know dad collected that sort of thing."

"Okay." He tapped the second X with the cap of his pen. "Next we have Sanlanda Sue's Hometown, which looks to be about a hundred miles or so south of SF."

"You seem to know California pretty well."

"Born there."

"What brought you East?"

"The pursuit of my career. What about Sue?"

"There's a mission in the town of San Orlando. When I was little, I couldn't pronounce that and called it Sanlanda instead. And so that became part of our family slang," she said. "One of the most illustrious citizens of the town, though not a lady I ever met myself, was Susan Pond. Better known as San Orlando Sue, she ran a whorehouse. One summer, when we were vacationing there, Shawn sneaked off and visited the place. It was his very first such experience and he eventually told me about it."

"So the town is San Orlando. But would this madam be likely to store a trunk of comic books for your brother?"

"I think he got to be friendly with Sue, years later. When he was roaming the country and possibly dealing drugs." She looked out at a road sign they were passing. "We're about five minutes from Buzz's house."

"The last X is down nearly to Los Angeles. Place called Whitehat City."

"Yes, once one of my favorite places." She reached into the glove compartment for a tissue and wiped her nose. "Whitehats are cowboys—the hero kind. Blackhats are the villains. The place is Hootman's Cowboy Ranch. Dan Hootman was briefly a cowboy in the movies, a singing cowboy who sang off-key. He opened the ranch right after the Second World War and it was used in lots of B-Westerns and dozens of TV shows. He shut it down in about nineteen sixty but kept on living there. My father and Dan were old friends and we used to visit there a lot. Cowboys were already fading from television when I was a kid, but I always liked them. I went through a phase of being fond of horses and that may account for part of it."

"Is Hootman still living there?"

"I don't know, but he always liked Shawn and he'd certainly store a trunk or two for him without asking questions."

Dan was frowning. "Even though you're the only one who knows what the names mean, the locations of these towns are in just about the right places on the map. Anybody who knows more than a little about California—or has access to an atlas—can figure that much out." He tore the page out of his sketchbook. "Even without a decoder, Buzz will be able to get to Clarinda and San Orlando and the ranch maybe."

"You're being hypercritical, not to mention excessively dippy," Sally pointed out, sounding falsely patient. "Look, if I drew a map that was the shape of Brimstone and put an X on it and labeled that 'Foible's ghost haunts this place' . . . could you find your way to your house from just that? I mean if you were Buzz and didn't know who you were?"

"If I knew that you and I were chums I might be able to—"

"I'm telling you that only my brother and I can decipher the personal code on that damn map."

"Maybe, but Buzz—and whoever the hell he may be in cahoots with—can sure get to the specific towns in question."

"The towns perhaps," she conceded, "but that's not close enough. It still gives us the edge."

"That doesn't mean he won't been lurking in these towns when we get there, ready to tail us as soon . . . Whoa, what is it? You look suddenly uneasy."

"Oh, nothing."

Jack asked her, "You never reminisced with Buzz about your childhood? You know, the way people do— never told the guy about Sanlanda and Uncle John and the whitehats versus the blackhats stuff?"

"All right, okay," she said, frowning. "It just occurred to me that I do tend to babble, especially sometimes in bed with people. I don't know, it is just maybe a possibility that I did talk to him about the winery and some of the other things."

Jack nodded. "One more reason to get westward fast."

Sally pulled off the road onto the edge of a grassy field. "I don't want to park any closer," she said. "Buzz's place is just around the next bend. He's not likely to be home, but we'd best sneak up on it anyway."

"A good idea." He folded up the map he'd drawn and started to deposit it in a jacket pocket.

Smiling, Sally took it from between his fingers and dropped it into her tan purse.

Chapter

7

The shooting didn't start until after they were inside Buzz Wisebecker's house.

With Sally in the lead, they'd come at the faded brown shingle ranch house from the rear, moving quietly and cautiously through the stand of white maples that separated Buzz's acre-and-a-half from the big estate next to it.

After crouching in the brush at the edge of the woods for several minutes and detecting no sign of movement in the house, they'd decided to go on in.

"C'mon." Sally rose up and started across the back lawn.

Jack got up and followed.

She slowed, glancing back at him. "What the heck was that creaking noise?"

"My bones." He caught up with her.

54

"How old are you anyway?"

"Not quite thirty-seven," he answered, "and old age has nothing to do with it. Being tied up on a concrete floor for most of the night will make even a spry teenager's skeleton a little squeaky the next day."

"Where'd you get that notion—from some article on bondage you read in *Penthouse?*"

"Common sense."

"Hooey." She sprinted ahead and climbed the low back porch. From her purse she took a jingling ring of keys. The first one she selected didn't fit. "Darn—ah, this is the proper one."

The weathered brown door opened inward and she followed it.

The shadowy hallway ran through the ranch house from back to front. It smelled strongly of old tobacco smoke, spilled beer, and spoiled food.

"Buzz must be using that new aftershave," commented Jack, trailing the young woman and sniffing at the stale air.

"Hush," she whispered.

They passed the kitchen first, on their left. All the drawers and cupboards were opened and silverware, pots, and crumpled grocery bags were scattered all over the yellow floor.

"Somebody's been here," said Sally, surveying the disorderly kitchen from the threshold. "Even Buzz isn't this slovenly."

"They were searching for something."

"I don't understand who exactly would . . . Whoops!" She had turned and was staring downhall.

A large, wide man had come popping out of an open doorway at the other end of the house. He wore a dark ski mask, a dark down jacket, dark jeans, and heavy lumberjack boots. He did a fast double take, like a bear in an animated cartoon, and scooted out of sight.

Sally grabbed hold of Jack's arm, hurried him across the corridor toward an open door. "Maybe we can—"

A second man, leaner and wearing a baggy orange-and-purple ski mask, emerged up ahead. He was ducked low and held a .38 revolver in his left hand. Without pausing to aim, he fired twice.

Both slugs missed.

By the time the echoes from the second shot had died, Sally and Jack were squatting in the closet in Buzz's bedroom.

"What are we doing here?" he asked her.

"Hiding," she whispered, putting an arm around him. "I think the game we're playing is actually called 'shooting fish in a barrel.'"

The sound of running feet grew louder out in the hall.

"I wish I hadn't left the church," said Sally, hugging him tighter. "At least I could pray in situations like this."

The thudding of heavy feet grew even louder and then started to fade.

The back door was yanked open, then slammed shut.

Sally sighed.

After a moment Jack disentangled himself from her and stepped clear of the closet. "Would this be where Buzz kept his suitcases?"

Getting up, she smoothed at her jeans and stepped into the bedroom. "Yes, and they're gone."

"Indicating that Buzz has taken off."

Sally sat down on the edge of the unmade bed. "Who were those goons who were searching his house?"

The bureau drawers had been tugged out and their contents dumped. "He sure kept a goodly supply of condoms on hand," Jack observed, wading through the debris. "Obviously somebody else is interested in the

Tijuana Bible and the loot. Unless those guys had an entirely different mission."

"But Buzz is the mastermind behind trying to steal the comic books."

"Mastermind isn't exactly the word I'd apply to him." He leaned on the doorway, watching her. "So it's possible, Sally, that he was working for someone else."

"You mean he maybe double-crossed whoever it was he was working for? Or should that be whomever?"

"Whichever, yes. It could be that once he got hold of the Tijuana Bible he decided to go out on his own," said Jack. "And whoever was backing him came looking for him and the map."

"Everything keeps getting more complex." She rubbed a thumb knuckle across her forehead. "The fellow who shot at us . . ."

"Yeah?"

"Darn, I hate even to mention this, considering the way Buzz has turned out."

"He wasn't another of your gentlemen friends?"

She placed her right hand on her left knee and watched it. "Well, I didn't actually recognize him," Sally said, talking chiefly toward the open closet. "But I did recognize the ski mask. I . . . um . . . I believe I knitted that about a year-and-a-half ago."

"That orange-and-purple thing?"

"That one, yes."

"For whom?"

She let her breath out slowly. "At the time I was dating—"

The door chimes sounded, bonging out loudly a fragment of a tune Jack didn't recognize. "Maybe somebody heard the shooting."

"Let's sit here quietly until they go away."

"Mr. Wisebecker? Miss Westerland? Is everything all

57

right in there?" someone was shouting out on the front porch.

A dog started barking.

Jack scowled at her. "You spend a lot of time here?"

"Some."

"I heard gunshots. Shall I phone the police?"

Sally popped up from the bed, crossed the bedroom, and pushed by Jack into the hall. "That's Mr. Niewenhaus," she explained, starting toward the front door. "He really will call the cops if I don't squelch him."

Jack followed in her wake. "Who is he?"

"Neighbor. A stockbroker I think. Jogs a lot, with his half-wit dog. . . . Well, good morning, Mr. Niewenhaus," she said, smiling, as she pulled the door open.

He was about fifty-five, fat and bearded, dressed in a brand-new maroon running suit. A fat dog the exact shade of peanut butter was trying to jump up at Sally, held back by a black leather leash.

"You're not shot?"

"Oh, that explosive noise," she said, smiling and making discouraging swats in the direction of the anxious dog. "Down, Moriarty."

"I was going to run on by, but then I decided I'd better not. I'm up to two miles every—"

"Congratulations, you're looking much trimmer. Well, thanks for stopping, it was thoughtful of—"

"I know I heard shots. In my younger days I was in the National Guard and I can—"

"Isn't it funny how some things sound exactly like gunshots and yet aren't gunshots," said Sally, laughing. "It fools even experts."

"What exactly was it that I heard," asked Niewenhaus, starting to frown and trying to look around the young woman and into the house through the slice of

58

open doorway, "that sounded exactly like gunshots and wasn't, Miss Westerland?"

"Well, let me see if I can explain this," she said, reaching behind her and grabbing hold of Jack's hand as a possible source of inspiration.

"Let's fess up, Sal," said Jack, opening the door wider and grinning broadly at the runner and his dog. "We may as well tell Mr. Niewenhaus the truth."

Moriarty began snarling, dropping his stubby tail and trying to lunge at Jack.

Sally began, "This is—"

"I'm Duncan Excalibur," said Jack, the grin widening. "You've probably seen me on Broadway or television. I've only made a handful of movies, so possibly you—"

"No." Niewenhaus was looking him over sceptically.

"Ah, fame," said Jack, chuckling. "At any rate, sir, we might as well confess—Sal and I—that we were rehearsing a scene from my . . . our next play. It's the one where Bernice comes home and finds Roger in the bedroom. She takes out the hidden gun that was used by Arthur to murder Aunt Nancy and fires at him twice."

"With real bullets?"

"No, of course not. We used blanks."

"Blanks don't sound like that."

"Actually they do, when you shoot them off in a ranch house with the particular acoustics of this one."

After eyeing both of them, Niewenhaus asked, "Where's Buzz Wisebecker?"

"At work," answered Sally. "He's at the Westport Artists School in Westport."

"At five-thirty A.M.?"

"That's how Buzz is," she replied. "Very gung ho."

"Duncan Excalibur," said Niewenhaus thoughtfully. "That name doesn't ring quite true to me."

"It's my stage name," explained Jack. "My real name is Butch Wisebecker. Buzz is my cousin."

Niewenhaus turned to Sally. "I'll take your word for what's been going on here, Miss Westerland," he said, reluctance evident in his voice. "But I think I'll drop in after work this evening and see what Mr. Wisebecker has to say."

"Do that. In fact, come for cocktails," she invited, smiling sweetly. "About sevenish."

"Fine. Come along, Moriarty."

The dog gave a parting snarl and went trotting off after his master.

Sally shut the door slowly and quietly and then leaned against it. "Duncan Excalibur?"

"It's the civilian name of Captain Vengeance, one of the superheroes Goldberg draws for Maximus Comics."

"I thought gag writers were good at thinking on their feet."

"I did think quickly, and thereby prevented him from calling the law down on us. And I didn't stand there batting my eyes at him and giggling, as—"

"Jesus, and you try to sell him the old rehearsing-a-play routine. That's so old and tired that—"

"It got rid of him."

"Maybe." Sally took a look out the spyhole in the door. "He's jogging away from here very slowly and with many a backward glance."

"All guys who weigh two hundred and fifty pounds jog slowly. It's a basic law of physics."

"I don't know, Jack. A man, fat or otherwise, who names his dog after a character in Sherlock Holmes may fancy himself an amateur detective."

"He probably named it after the bartender in his favorite saloon in Manhattan. Almost half of them are named Moriarty," said Jack. "But we'd better get out of here right now."

"That's a good suggestion." She started for the back door.

"You were going to tell me the name of one of the gunmen," he reminded, catching up with her.

"I made the ski mask for Walt Murchison," she said. "But that couldn't have been him."

"Was he built like him?"

"More or less, yes—and Walt is left-handed."

"So, why can't it be Walt Murchison?"

"Well, he worked for W.A.S. up until about six months ago," she said, reaching for the doorknob. "But I can't see any reason he'd be searching Buzz's house— or trying to shoot me."

Chapter

8

––––––––––––––––––––

Fagin, who hadn't shaved in three days or more, was crawling along the linoleum floor of his diner and spraying cockroach poison along the baseboards. "You two look like you came straight here from the motel, Deacon," he observed as Jack and Sally entered.

Pointing down at the proprietor, Jack grinned and said, "This is the quaint ambiance I was telling you about."

"You're already too late for the breakfast specials." Fagin crawled into an empty booth, spray can hissing.

"I'm growing rather fond of the funereal scent of that stuff," said Goldberg when they joined him in the usual booth. "Neither this pesthole nor Fagin has smelled this good in weeks. You must be Sally." He stood, bowed, and sat again. There was a plate of waffles on the table in front of him.

Smiling, she sat opposite the lean comic-book artist. "Jack says I can trust you."

"Gee, no woman has applied the word trustworthy to me since the Carter administration," he said. "But, yeah, you can."

Jack slid in next to her, enjoying the proximity. "Can you take a quick look at something, Lew—a list of old comic books?"

"Sure," he said. "You really did get here late today, Jack. What exactly has happened since last we spoke?"

Sally thrust her hand into her tan purse and came out with several folded sheets of manila typing paper. She passed them to Goldberg. "This is a partial list of my father's collection. He typed it up himself about six years ago, Lew. I penciled in some tentative prices maybe two years back. You can tell him what happened last night and this morning, Jack."

"Not if it's going to make me blush." Lew took the list but didn't open it.

"Well," said Jack, "it all began . . ." He gave Goldberg a fairly concise account of what had taken place at Sally's house from the time he'd arrived to deliver the Tijuana Bible. He then outlined what had befallen them when they dropped by Buzz Wisebecker's place.

"*Caramba,* as my old Yiddisher grandmother used to say," observed Goldberg when Jack finished. "Life does indeed imitate Maximus Comics."

"Is this a meeting of the Civil Liberties Union?" inquired Fagin from across the diner. "Or are you going to order something for you and your doxie, Deacon?"

"Two coffees," he said without turning around, "to start."

Fagin glared at the thin waitress huddled behind the counter. "Into action, Marie."

Goldberg unfurled the list of the Westerland collection. "Yikes," he remarked after scanning the top sheet for a few seconds. "This isn't a joke?"

"Nope, dad had them all."

"What's the condition?—that's important. Ratty, bedraggled, not so bad, pristine mint?"

"Almost all of them were in excellent condition—fine to excellent."

Nodding, he sighed and glanced at the ceiling. "Well, just to consider this run of *Action Comics*— He has every issue from number one to a hundred twelve, huh?"

"He was missing fifteen."

"Even so—and this is without consulting a price guide—Sally, the prices you estimated are far too modest." He hunched slightly, studied the list again. "If you sold just these hundred and some issues of *Action*, depending on how you marketed them, you'd realize at least twenty-five thousand and maybe as much as forty thousand dollars. Superman fans and speculators dote on this title." Swiftly Goldberg flipped through the remaining pages of the list. "Oy! *New Fun Comics* number one through number seven—*Marvel Mystery* number two through number forty—*Whiz* number two through number seventy—and a ton of Disney titles. And so on and so on." He dropped the list, reverentially, next to his plate. "At a rough guess I'd say the whole collection has to be worth at least two-million dollars, Sally."

"Caramba," said Jack.

"What are you lying about now, Goldberg?" inquired the thin waitress as she set down two cups of coffee.

"Oh, merely how much I expect to earn drawing comic books this year, sweet."

"Two million, huh?" She took a step back and surveyed him. "That's almost enough money to make you tolerable."

"What did I warn you about fraternizing, Marie?" called Fagin from in front of the grill.

She hurried away from the booth.

Sally rested an elbow on the table. "Our main problem, Lew, is that we don't actually have the comic books right at the moment."

"That's a pity. Where are they?"

"Well, my brother borrowed them from my father—and he seems to have hidden them in various spots out in California."

Goldberg sat up straight, snapped his fingers, and smiled. "The Old Poontang Mine."

"Yep, that's what the map is about," said Jack. "It shows three possible spots where the comics might be, stored in steamer trunks."

"Or at least they were in trunks when I saw them last," said Sally, trying her coffee. "My lord, that's vile."

"Right, it's an old Fagin family recipe." Goldberg drummed his fingertips on the edge of the plate. "It occurs to me, Jack, after attending attentively to your narrative of recent events, that you've got competition for this treasure trove."

"There's Buzz, who's got the original of the map," said Jack, nodding in agreement. "Plus another group— the goons who shot at us at his house. That may include a fellow named Walt Murchison."

"Murchison? A second-rate inker," said Goldberg. "They threw him off *Little Billy Billions* up at Maximus a couple of years ago. Replaced him with an orangutan with the shakes and the stuff looks much better now."

Sally frowned at Jack. "All we know for certain is that the man at Buzz's was wearing Walt's ski mask."

Goldberg said, "Let's move from haberdashery to another point. Which of these louts killed Mutt Shermer?"

Sally said forlornly, "That killing has to involve Buzz.

65

Since he's the only one who knew poor Mutt might be at my old cottage."

"Back at that point in time," put in Jack, "Buzz and Walt could've still been partners."

Goldberg said, "And they didn't fall out until Buzz absconded with the Tijuana Bible, huh?"

"That seems logical."

"This is all very disheartening." Sally pushed her cup farther away from her. "I mean, we're sitting here trying to decide which of my former beaus is a murderer."

"They could both be," said Jack. "Buzz and Walt may both have tortured Mutt to get him to tell them more about the hidden comic books."

"We don't know if that's what killed him," reminded Goldberg. He picked up his fork and started cutting his waffle into quarters. "Maybe he was knifed or shot."

"There were gunshots," reminded Sally.

"What's needed is a body," said Goldberg. "If Mutt's remains would show up, then the identity of his killer would be a lot easier to establish." He cut each quarter in half. "Has it, by the way, occurred to either of you madcaps that people who don't mind wiping out old rumdum cartoonists like Mutt can also kill clean-cut, upwardly mobile types such as yourselves?"

"Certainly," said Sally. "But those comics are *mine.* I mean to get them back."

Goldberg nodded at his friend. "And you?"

"I'm going along," Jack answered. "Sally and I are partners in this."

"Equal partners?"

Jack picked up his coffee cup and took an unenthusiastic sip. "Not exactly."

"Were I risking *my* life, I'd want at least half of all—"

"We ought to arrange to get ourselves on a flight to California, Jack."

66

Jack inquired, "Does Midge still run that travel agency in Wilton, Lew?"

He lowered his forkful of waffle. "Imagine any rational person marrying a woman who'd allow herself to be called Midge."

"Who's Midge?" asked Sally.

"Goldberg's ex-wife."

"Imagine my having to say that name night after night in romantic tones for three-and-a-half long years. 'Midge.'" He shook the fork negatively, causing the chunk of waffle to go flying away.

"No food fights in here," warned Fagin.

Jack said, "You and Midge are on good terms still, aren't you?"

"As good terms as our mutual loathing will allow. Why?"

"We need to get booked on a flight to San Francisco. No later than early this evening if possible."

"Any travel agency can do that. Why drag in my former—"

"But not every agency can find out for us what flight Buzz Wisebecker took and where he was bound."

Goldberg contemplated the ceiling again. "Okay, I'll degrade myself for the sake of friendship," he said at last. "I'll call her for you. Want me to check on the peregrinations of Walt Murchison, too?"

"You'd better, yeah. Also see if you can find out if either of them is traveling with anyone."

"Especially," added Sally, "anyone built along the lines of a grizzly bear."

Goldberg gazed at his waffle. "Should I phone her on an empty stomach or fortify myself?"

Leaning closer to Jack, Sally asked him, "Is Lew also the one who's going to help finance our—"

"Eh?" Goldberg cupped a hand to his ear. "Wait now,

friends. I don't mind suffering humiliation and verbal abuse at the hands of my erstwhile spouse, but I won't loan anybody any money."

Jack grinned. "I have someone else in mind," he said, standing and starting to frisk himself. "I'll go phone. Got a dime?"

Goldberg fished one out of his pants pocket. "This is the limit of my financing of this expedition," he said, flipping it off his thumb to his friend.

Chapter

9

The airliner was moving westward across the night.

Returning to her aisle seat, Sally nudged Jack and quietly said, "Don't get the notion that I'm paranoid, but I noticed somebody when I was coming back from the john."

Jack was sitting stiffly in the window seat, his sketchbook open to a blank page and resting on his meal tray. "Not somebody else you knitted a hat for?"

"No, but someone I'm pretty sure I've seen before."

"A friend of Buzz's?"

"I don't think so. Not a close friend or he'd have been invited to one of those godawful parties Buzz was always having and I'd have met him that way."

"Somebody you've seen hanging around the Westport Artists School maybe?"

"Don't think so." Sally settled into her seat, opened

the copy of the fat paperback, *The Official Overstreet Comic Book Price Guide*, that Goldberg had given them as a going-away gift. "He's six rows back on our side of the plane, in an aisle seat. Thin, blond, about forty—he looks something like that actor, you know, who fell off the Statue of Liberty in the Hitchcock movie. Tan suit that doesn't fit him all that well. Of course, Norman Lloyd."

"That's his name?"

"No, that's the name of the actor he looks like," Sally said. "Maybe you ought to go back and take a look, see if you recognize him."

"In a while."

She eyed him. "You don't enjoy flying, do you?"

"Flying is okay. It's crashing that unsettles me."

"I love flying. We always flew out to California on our vacations, except once when we took the train because my father thought we'd see more of the country that way. What he forgot was that railroad tracks never pass through the nicer parts of towns."

"Poor little rich girl."

"What's that mean?"

"Nothing. Well, almost nothing. The house I grew up in was about a block from the tracks—on the wrong side."

"Maybe we went by your house when I was a kid."

"No, I wouldn't have forgotten you," he said. "I'll go check him out in a few minutes."

Sally said, "There's no way anyone could know we were catching this flight from JFK."

Jack said, "Unless they did the same thing we did to find out that Buzz had taken off for San Francisco this morning."

"Darn, we should've used aliases."

"Does this guy you spotted seem to be alone?"

"There's a fat lady of about seventy dozing in the seat next to him. She's not my idea of an accomplice."

"We ought to be able to dodge a single tail."

"All of this really makes me mad," she said. "I'm the sole heir to those comic books, damn it. Nobody else has any right to them."

"Keep in mind that Wally Warfield now owns five percent of whatever they bring."

She nodded, cheek puckering. "I think it's great that you got your boss to—"

"I assist Wally on *Freddie Foible*, but he's not exactly—"

"Hey, I'm not trying to put you down, Jack. I think it's marvelous that you got Wally to advance us five thousand dollars for expenses."

"Working for a multimillionaire has its advantages," he said. "Besides, he was a good friend of your father and he likes you."

"Of course five percent of our take could be as much as a hundred thousand."

"Or it could be nothing."

"I think we could've got Wally for two percent tops."

"Okay, next time we go on a half-assed scavenger hunt together, Sally, you dig up the goddamn—"

"I'm not criticizing you. Maybe your delusion that you grew up on the wrong side of the tracks is making you suspect—"

"I'll show you the tracks while we're out there. Real tracks, real wrong side."

"Do you know what *Batman* number one is worth?"

"Is this a subtle attempt to change the subject?"

"Yes."

"Okay, what?"

"Well, Overstreet—whoever he may be—gives prices for three conditions. Good, fine, and mint. Now

71

good is twelve hundred dollars, fine is thirty-six hundred, and mint is eighty-four hundred," she said, squinting at the open page in the price guide. "I figure my father's copy is better than fine. So that's five thousand right there. And our number two should bring at least fifteen hundred. On the run of *Batman* alone we'll take in—"

"You ought to keep in mind that comic books are printed on cheap paper," he reminded her. "Sitting around in trunks and being trundled all over the country may've futzed up their condition."

"Dad kept each issue in a specially treated plastic bag."

"Sure, but your brother may've unpacked them and dumped them in cardboard cartons or gunny sacks. They may be moldering in somebody's damp, rat-infested cellar."

"That's a more negative view than I care to take."

"I just don't want to see you disappointed if we find them in less than—"

"I intend to enjoy the quest as much as the finding of the treasure," she told him. "So screw you, Dr. Doom."

He smiled. "This is my first treasure hunt," he said. "Could be I'm too pessimistic."

She turned ahead in the price guide. "*Superman* number one," she said. "Good is thirty-two hundred, fine is ninety-five hundred, and mint is—wow!—twenty thousand dollars. Our copy has to be worth at least fifteen thousand, I'd estimate."

"Providing you can get somebody to pay that. It could be this Overstreet is just guessing that—"

"No, no. This book is all done scientifically—by consulting dealers and collectors all over the place and so on," she assured him. "Trust me, Jack, when we get the comic books, there will be plenty of customers who'll pay these prices or better. We may even be able to auction some of the more expensive ones and realize even more."

"I'll go view the blond gent." After thinking about it for several seconds he was able to stand up, ease around her and into the aisle.

He started walking slowly toward the restrooms at the rear of the plane. He struggled not to contemplate the fact that he was something like thirty thousand feet in the air, but he found himself thinking about it. That caused his legs to get rubbery and he reached out suddenly to steady himself against a seat back.

Missing the seat, he clutched someone's shoulder. "Excuse me, I—"

"That's okay. I get shaky when I fly, too."

Jack was clutching the blond man in the tan suit.

He produced a false grin, let go, and continued on to the rear. Jack didn't recognize the man and was certain he'd never seen him before.

"He doesn't even look like the actor in the Hitchcock movie," he said to himself as he reached for the sliding handle of the restroom door.

An odd sound awakened him. Jack opened his eyes gradually, yawned, and discovered that Sally was asleep with her head against his chest and her right arm tight around him. The sound was the beating of her heart.

He hadn't awakened this close to a woman for quite some time. After the departure of his wife, Jack had moped a lot and concentrated on saving himself from financial ruin. Dating hadn't played much of a part in his life. And until he'd opened his closet and found Sally there, he really hadn't encountered a woman who much interested him.

There was a pain running from his left cheekbone down as far as his lowest rib, his knees felt numb, and his toes felt as though they were trying to retract into his feet. Yet he was in a fine mood.

"Shawn, don't . . ." Sally lifted her head with a jerk, shook it a few times. "Nightmare, sorry." Slowly she sat up and away from him. Reaching down, she located her purse on the floor and brought it up.

"Good morning," he said. "You okay?"

"Sure, I often wake up screaming these days." She got out her compact and took a look at herself in the mirror. "If we were on our way to auditions for *The Bride of Frankenstein,* I'd be a cinch for the part."

He shifted in his seat, his bones producing creaks. "Since Buzz was landing in San Francisco, that means he could've headed either for the wine country or Mission San Orlando."

"I decided I want to try Uncle John first." She brushed at her long blond hair with her free hand. "Did your wife look gorgeous in the morning?"

"Not especially."

"Some women can wake up and look immediately terrific," she said as she applied her lipstick. "Me, I tend to look as though I've been sleeping in a skid-row alley with my face on a rusty waffle iron."

"Is this the part in the scene where I'm supposed to say, 'Why, Sal, you're a real beaut'?"

"Why so grouchy?"

"You're a very pretty woman, we both know it. You don't have to angle for—"

"Thanks." She shut the compact. "After a few months with Buzz, maybe I simply want to have somebody pay me some obvious compliments again."

"I'll work on it."

She asked, "What was your wife's name?"

"Mrs. Deacon."

"Her first name."

"It escapes me at the moment."

74

"Now who's acting?"

Jack said, "After she left I figured I didn't want to talk about her much anymore."

"Do you love her?"

"Nope."

"Did you."

"I must've once."

"How'd she feel about you?"

"Never mentioned it."

"What's the admiral look like?"

"I have no idea."

"When you think about them, how do you visualize the man?"

"I see Danny DeVito in the part."

She said, "It really hurt you, her running off like that."

He glanced out the airliner window. "It did, yeah."

"But didn't you maybe also feel—well, somewhat relieved?"

"Is that how you feel about Buzz?"

Smiling briefly, Sally answered, "Yes, it is. He was, in many ways, a pain in the butt."

"About that blond guy who may possibly be trailing us," he said.

"He really *does* look a lot like Norman Lloyd. You know, he was also on 'St. Elsewhere.'"

"Whatever he looks like, we ought to try to ditch him."

"I've been thinking about that," she said. "What we'll do is collect our luggage and then go into one of the cocktail lounges at the airport."

"Sort of early for that."

"Exactly," said Sally.

———

"There," said Sally, "that proves it."

"May only prove that the guy's an alcoholic."

"No, he ordered a club soda, just like us. Nobody craves that."

75

There were less than a dozen people scattered around the large, black-walled cocktail lounge at the San Francisco International Airport. Jack and Sally were in a black imitation-leather booth near the padded black door and the blond man was across the room sitting on a stool at the bar, the attaché case that was his only baggage sitting on the floor near a back leg of his stool.

Sally took a sip of her club soda. "He is definitely following us."

"Okay, it does seem like he is."

She gathered up her purse. "I'm going to pretend to visit the bathroom," she announced quietly.

"And what are you actually going to be doing?"

"You just remain calm, no matter what. And be ready to snatch up our suitcases and depart."

"Sally?"

She smiled, slid gracefully free of their booth. Bending, she kissed him on the cheek. "Domestic camouflage," she said and walked away from him.

"Why do I keep falling in love with lunatics?" he asked himself. He opened his sketchbook, took a pen out of his breast pocket. "Let's see . . . Freddie is packing for a trip . . . he loses his luggage at an airport . . . he has to go buy a new suitcase . . . salesman tells him this one is so strong an elephant can't crush it . . . Freddie just happens to have an elephant with him and wants to test it . . . no, not right . . . it's so tough a gorilla can't crush it . . . a gorilla can dance on it . . . gorilla comes in and dances on it, with straw hat and cane . . . naw, too hokey . . ." He looked up from his doodling.

The blond shadow was still at the bar, nursing his drink. Sally was nowhere in sight.

Jack chewed thoughtfully on the cap of his pen. "Freddie brings all his clothes and sports equipment to the luggage shop to make sure he gets a suitcase to fit it all . . . not quite right . . . it's so strong an elephant can step on it and not crush it . . . he buys it and on the way home an elephant steps on it and crushes it . . . Freddie takes it back to the shop and asks for a refund . . . not bad, but Wally'll want to know where the elephant came from . . ."

The padded door of the cocktail lounge slowly opens. Two uniformed men, one of them black, came slowly and carefully in. Halting, with hands near their holsters, they scanned the scatter of early-morning bar patrons. After a quiet exchange of words, they moved, in slow lockstep, over to the bar.

The black man tapped the shoulder of the blond shadow.

"Pssst."

Pete turned and saw Sally in the doorway.

She motioned for him to join her and bring the baggage.

Nodding, he tucked his sketchbook and pen away and gathered up the two medium-sized suitcases. Looking as innocent as he could, he left the booth and slow-footed to the doorway and out.

In the main reception area he asked Sally, "Did you arrange that?"

She smiled, took her suitcase, and hurried him along with a hand on his arm. "I also rented us a car. It's only an eighty-seven Isuzu, but we got a terrific rate."

"What did you tell the airport police—that he was tailing us?"

"*I* didn't tell them a darn thing," she explained. "But a very nervous and upset young woman with a thick Middle East accent phoned them to confess that she'd had second thoughts. She was feeling contrite and wanted them to know that her American terrorist lover was planning to blow up the next flight to Disneyland."

"And they believed you?"

"Hey, I'm an actress, remember? Character voices aren't my specialty, but I wasn't bad. When I told them he had the explosives in his attaché case, it played very well."

———

They were five miles from the airport and heading for the city of San Francisco, with Jack driving, when he noticed the green car in the rearview. After watching it off and on for a moment, he said, "Somebody's following us."

"You sure?"

"Pretty much so."

"But Norman Lloyd's still tangled up with the airport cops. He can't be tailing us, Jack."

"I can't get that clear a look at the driver," he told her. "But I think it's that fat old lady who was sitting next to him on the plane."

Chapter

10

Sally was sitting sideways in the passenger seat beside him, looking intently out the rear window. "It's a Toyota."

"That's good to know."

"Well, it seems to me, Jack, that the more we know about them, the better—"

"Them?"

"There's a man in the front seat with the old lady," she explained, facing front again.

"It isn't the blond guy from the plane?"

"Do you want me to describe him? When I tried to tell you about the car, you—"

"If the car had run over me, or even my dog, then the fact that it's a Toyota might be of interest," he said. "When, however, it's chasing us along a freeway—"

"He's a skinny man with lots of red hair. A beard to match."

"You know any redheaded men?"

"None resembling this one."

"Their car's still about four cars behind us."

"Make that three."

Jack suddenly swung their car from the middle lane to the righthand lane. As several horns honked, he gunned it and went roaring onto an off-ramp. "We'll try to shake them."

"San Raffetto?" she said, reading the sign they were rushing by. "I've never been here."

"A bedroom town," he said, glancing into the rear-view mirror. "They've turned off, too."

"You know, that fat old lady . . ." Sally twisted a strand of hair around her finger.

"What about her?"

"I've been wondering if I hadn't seen her somewhere before."

"Back in Connecticut?" They reached the end of the off-ramp. He braked, waited for the light to change, and then turned left toward the town.

"Yes, except she wasn't an old lady then."

"What was she?"

"A man named Hoffman."

Jack speeded up, made it through a changing light, and swung right onto a side street that was lined with laundromats, cafes, and two small pharmacies. "You're telling me the old bimbo is a guy in drag?"

"I didn't even recognize him at first, when I saw him sitting next to the blond man on the airplane. Stands to reason, since I wasn't used to seeing Hoffman dressed like a granny."

"Who is he in everyday life?" He took the car swiftly around another corner. "Ah, they're losing ground." He gunned the Isuzu, sent it speeding around another cor-

80

ner, and then drove right into a used-car lot and parked it among the sale cars. "Saw this once on 'The Rockford Files.' Duck down."

Sally obliged. "Actually it was 'Harry-O.'"

"No, because Harry-O rarely drove a car. His was always in the garage and he rode the bus." Jack risked a quick look up over the edge of the door on his side. "They're going on by."

"About Hoffman," she said. "He's a buddy of Buzz's. He was only at one party, about three weeks ago. He told me he was a certified public accountant."

"An interesting blend of professions, CPA and drag queen."

"Are they slowing?"

"Nope, they're all the way down at the next corner, stopped at the signal."

"Maybe we've shaken them."

"Maybe, for now."

"Buzz must've been setting me up for this for quite a while."

"If he's always been intent on getting hold of the comic books, how'd he find out about them?"

Sally said, "I told him."

"How'd that come about?"

"Before we'd officially started dating, I had lunch with him and the subject of old comic books came up, how they were valuable and all. So I told him that my dad had put together a large collection."

"Sounds like he actually brought it up himself, to get you to talk. Indicating he already knew about the collection."

"But not that many people knew about it, Jack. And after Shawn made off with it, we didn't talk about it much with anyone."

"Name some who did know."

"Well, my brother obviously and Mutt Shermer," she

replied, "and Jarrett Cobb. Dad would show it to him now and then when he visited the house. That was the big house we used to own in Southport."

"The W.A.S. operation isn't doing that well."

"No, as I told you. We're getting deeper and deeper in the hole."

"So Cobb could use two million bucks."

"He could, sure. And he's a scoundrel and a sleaze, but he wouldn't try to rob his partner's daughter."

"Why not?"

She thought about his question. "Now that you mention it, I don't know why he wouldn't."

"Could be Cobb put Buzz up to approaching you about the comics. Suggested he romance you and find out if you knew where they were."

"Yes, he could've."

"Then Cobb might be the mastermind who's—"

The door on Jack's side jerked open.

Sally cried out.

A large dark man in a Hawaiian shirt, blue denims, and a tan Stetson was glowering at them. "Explain this to me," he requested. "You two doing drugs, having sex, contemplating knocking off my safe—or none of the above?"

Clearing his throat and sitting up, Jack said, "Actually our reason for parking here is fairly interesting, Mr. . . ."

"I'm Cowboy Karpinsky. Don't you see my spots on TV?"

"Cowboy," said Sally, in a soft, Southern belle voice, "you just look the sort of little old sweetheart who'll understand our plight."

"I'm a sweetheart, yeah."

"Well, you see Rupe and I . . ." She straightened up, smiling at him. "This here is Rupe, my boyhood beau. It

82

was in Atlanta that I first met the colonel and my old parents decided that I must marry him instead of—"

"Atlanta? I spent two years there and you sure don't have an Atlanta accent."

She laughed musically. "Well, isn't that perceptive of you? Isn't that smart of Cowboy, Rupe? I mean, here you up and knew right away that my parents had just about dragged me kicking and screaming to Atlanta to introduce me to the colonel." She smiled more broadly at him. "I just bet you can guess where I come from."

"Sounds more like Memphis."

"Well, Bingo." Sally laughed and clapped her hands together. "You hit it right on the nose. Anyway, Cowboy, it was just today that Rupe succeeded in tracking me to the mansion out here in California where the colonel's been holding me against my will with the help of several big nasty servants. We just now escaped, but they been chasing us. You probably saw them go racing by in that bulletproof Mercedes."

"I missed that." Karpinsky took off his Stetson and slapped it against his thigh. "If they try to give you any trouble, miss, I got a shotgun in my office."

"Isn't that helpful of him, Rupe?"

"It certainly is," said Jack. "But now, dear, we better think about getting away before they come back this way hunting for us."

"By the way," said the car dealer, "if it'll help you out any I can give you two thousand bucks for this wreck you're driving."

"We need it," said Jack, "but thanks for the offer." Gingerly he shut the door and started the engine.

"Thank you ever so much, Cowboy," said Sally, giving him a shy, fluttery wave.

He put his Stetson back on and then tipped it at her. "Glad to oblige, miss."

83

Jack drove out onto the street and started driving back in the direction of the freeway.

"How was I?" asked Sally, hugging herself and glancing back at the car lot.

"Karpinsky was touched."

"But you didn't like it?"

"Right now I want to concentrate on getting us to Sonoma County safely." He hunched slightly at the wheel.

"I think I was darn good, especially since I had to ad-lib all the dialogue."

"You were good."

"Then why are you miffed?"

"I'm not," he insisted.

Chapter

11

The town of Clarinda is approximately sixty miles
north of San Francisco. You can usually drive there in
about an hour-and-a-half.

It took Jack and Sally two hours and twenty minutes.
That was chiefly because Sally was driving and she
made several side trips off the main road to make certain they were no longer being pursued.

As she pulled off the main street of town and into
the large parking area next to the Old Clarinda Inn, the
white gravel on the lot rattled and splattered under
the car.

Jack awoke and sat up, dropping the sketchbook
from his lap to the floor. "Hum?"

"We've arrived," Sally announced, sliding the car into
a space. "Do you always wake up this groggy?"

He sat thoughtfully for a few seconds, then unbuckled his seatbelt and reached down to retrieve the book. "Did you happen to notice if I came up with any *Freddie Foible* gags while I was in my trance state?"

"Not a one." She eased out of the car, smoothing her plaid skirt. "Why don't you just look on this as a vacation and not try to work, Jack?"

He tucked the sketchbook away in a coat pocket and got out of the car. "Apparently I didn't mention all the conditions Wally set before letting me go on this excursion with you."

"Is one of them that you have to keep doing the strip?"

"No, not the actual strip—I just have to keep sending him gag ideas."

She'd turned her back to him and was looking, hands on hips, toward a silver-and-black van that was parked some two hundred yards away. It had *Anders-Fulson Productions* lettered on its side in discreet white. "That's interesting," she muttered.

"What is?"

"Oh, it's just someone I used to know."

"Someone of a dangerous sort?"

She shook her head. "How many ideas do you have to send to Wally?"

"Fifty."

"How many do you have so far?"

"Nine. Or possibly only seven."

"I think," she said, nodding in the direction of the inn, "that we better stay here and use it as our base of operations."

"Won't Uncle John put us up?"

"He would, but I don't want to go rushing in there," she told him. "Better bring our stuff."

Jack obliged and got the two suitcases out of the backseat. "It's a quaint old place."

The Old Clarinda Inn was a sprawling, three-story

building, a wooden structure in the Victorian style, painted white and rich with gingerbread trim, spires, and cupolas.

"According to the guide book, it was built three years ago," she said, starting for the white veranda.

"So it's not part of your cherished childhood memories of the town."

"Not at all." She climbed the wide wooden steps. "We'd better be Mr. and Mrs. Deacon here. It's easier to explain—and that way you can put the bill on your Visa, since mine's running low."

Jack cleared his throat. "Fine," he said, following her into the immense lobby.

———

Jack was sitting in the bentwood rocker next to the wide, canopied bed. "You don't want to call Uncle John first?" he said toward the half-open bathroom door.

The sink water ceased running. "Suppose somebody has their phones tapped?"

"You think Buzz is running that elaborate an operation?"

"It's not just him," she reminded, appearing in the doorway. She was wearing jeans again and a candystriped shirt. "We've got Hoffman, the blond man, the bear, and someone who may or may not be Walt Murchison. Not to mention that son of a bitch, Jarrett Cobb."

"Okay, we'll just drive out there—or rather we'll drive by the Macri Brothers Winery first. Then if things look safe, we'll go on into the grounds and look up Giovanni Macri."

She tied her hair back with the black ribbon. "I suppose we should've rushed right out there—but I really felt in need of a shower."

"Being tied up overnight in a basement has a way of making you feel a bit seedy."

Sally came into the bedroom. "Do you want to take a—"

"Nope, I'll go on being seedy until we check out the winery."

"I really appreciate all—"

The phone on the bedside table rang.

Jack stood up suddenly, frowned at it, and then looked across at Sally.

She shrugged, spreading her hands wide.

He picked up the receiver. "Hello?"

"Is Sally Westerland there?" asked a soft masculine voice.

"Who's calling?"

"Well, who exactly am I talking to?"

"A friend of the family—who are you?"

"This happens to be Gil Fulson."

Jack said to Sally. "Gil Fulson—is that the guy with the fancy van?"

Smiling, she came over and took the phone from him. "Hi, Gil. Nice of you to phone."

"Ah, it *is* you, sweet. I thought I saw you traipsing across the lobby with some lunkhead awhile ago, but my eyes are in just terrible shape because of an allergic reaction to all the goddamn nature in the raw hereabouts. Wouldn't you know it, we're up here to film a commercial and I'm absolutely and totally blind just about. That clunk you're with isn't actually your hubby, is he? Say nay."

"Don't worry, Gil. We're only shacking up," she explained. "Where are you doing this commercial?"

"At some dreadful old gothic pile that calls itself the Macri Brothers Winery. They have a process for dying horse piss red and calling it wine. We convinced them that Anders-Fulson would add a touch of class to their abysmal commercials."

"When are you due at the winery?"

"I'm supposed to make my initial inspection of the place this very afternoon, sweet. Though I'd much rather spend the time with you, talking about the good old days when you did those marvelous spots for Aberration perfume. It's a pity we can't use you on this shoot, Sally dearest. The creature Anders has hired has all the grace of a drunken zeppelin."

"We can get together, Gil, and you can—if you will—do me an enormous favor."

"Marvelous. What say we meet in the overblown lobby in fifteen minutes?"

"That'll be fine, but I'll have to bring the lunkhead along." She hung up, then poked Jack in the upper arm. "C'mon, clunk."

Gil Fulson was a large, broad-shouldered black man of forty-one. He had part of the rear of his van done up as a parlor. And there was a large one-way window built into the side. "Isn't that amazing" he was saying from the striped loveseat he was sprawled on, "that you actually help draw *Freddie Foible*, Jack? I absolutely adore that comic—it's so delightfully dumb. It never fails to give me a laugh. Don't you adore it, too, Sally?"

"Yes, I'm especially fond of the cockroach motif." She and Jack were sharing a small clawfoot sofa.

The van hit a bump in the street and the Tiffany lamp next to the loveseat rattled briefly. "You're not in some sort of terrible danger, are you, sweet?" he asked, scowling in the direction of his driver.

"Not exactly."

89

"But using my van as a sort of Trojan horse to get you unobtrusively onto the winery grounds—that smacks of intrigue."

"Later," promised Sally, "I'll try to explain all this to you, Gil."

"Oh, it makes no difference to me." He took a tissue out of a pocket of his tight-fitting jeans and blew his nose. "I'm so fond of duplicity and masquerading, that it doesn't really matter what your reasons are. The play's the thing, sweet."

They were moving along the main street of the town, passing its shops and restaurants—The Arbor Boutique, Vine's Café, The Sweater Pavilion, Monograms, Unlimited, The Thistle—Golfing Attire, Jack B. Nimble's Candle Shoppe, The Sweat Sock—Sports Attire, The Wine Barrel—Dining Experience.

"Changed a lot," observed Sally.

"Gentrification has struck," said Gil, sneezing. "It's spreading all across the golden state like a blight. A very expensive blight, of course."

"That used to be a hardware store," Sally said to Jack, pointing. "Right next to it was an ice cream parlor, one that'd been there for years. Shawn and I loved to . . . Well, that was years ago and it's over and done."

"I don't suppose," asked Gil, leaning forward, "that you could get me a *Freddie* original, Jack? I'd really love to frame one and hang it in my LA office."

"Sure, just give me your card and I'll . . . Oops!" He stood, nodding toward the street they were driving on.

Sally saw him, too, coming out of a studiously old-fashioned pharmacy. "The blond man," she said.

Gil glanced in that direction. "Someone I know?"

"No," said Sally. "Just another old friend of mine."

———

Gil opened the rear door of his van and gazed into the bright afternoon. "Imagine me journeying to this wilderness to make a commercial about a product called MacKooler wine cooler." Sighing deeply, sneezing twice, he dropped to the ground.

"Doesn't seem to be anyone suspicious lurking around." Sally stepped out.

"But the blond guy is back in town." Jack followed her. "So eventually he's likely to find his way here."

"That's why we've got to get to Uncle John right away."

They were in the visitors' parking lot. About a quarter of a mile away were three buildings that housed the winery's offices and living quarters, gray stone structures that resembled small, squat castles. Beyond the buildings stretched a couple of acres of neat-cropped grass and then came the vineyards. The afternoon sky was a clear, cloudless blue.

Gil sneezed again. "They must have air conditioning somewhere in this outback outpost."

"C'mon," said Sally. "I'll escort you to Giovanni Macri's office."

"Imagine that old curmudgeon being a longtime chum of yours, Sally, and even a pleasant fixture of your childhood," said the commercial director. "He struck me as the sort who trained kids to pick pockets and steal gents' handkerchiefs."

"You've met him?"

"Only via the telephone, while he was trying to browbeat me into lowering the already suicidally low price Anders had quoted him for immortalizing this swill of his on film." The big black man shuddered. "MacKooler—even the winos on skid row shun the stuff."

Sally put her arm through Jack's. "It seems to be peaceful enough around here."

"On the surface." The three of them walked across the graveled lot toward the middle castle.

91

"I don't understand how the blond man found his way to Clarinda."

"Somebody told him it was probably one of the towns on the map."

Sally said, "Yes, I suppose Buzz could've done that."

"You know, you two, I'm starting to feel terribly left out," complained Gil. "I don't, really, have a notion of what you're chattering about."

"I'm sorry, Gil," she said as they climbed the stone steps of the Macri Brothers Winery building. "I'll write you a long explanatory letter as soon as we get everything worked out."

"Sweet, you never write letters. I'm still waiting for the note telling me you got home safely to Connecticut after we shot those spots down in Bermuda two years ago."

"I actually sent it. Must've gone astray."

The large oval reception lobby was chill.

"Ah, air conditioning," sighed Gil. He went striding over to the slim, dark-haired young woman behind the oaken desk. "I happen to be Gil Fulson. Mr. Giovanni Macri's anxiously awaiting me."

"Oh, yes, Mr. Fulson." She smiled up at him. "And who are these two others?"

"Associates," he explained. "I rarely travel without an entourage."

She stood. "You'll find Mr. Macri in that office marked Executive in Chief," she said, nodding. "Just across the lobby there."

Beckoning to Jack and Sally, Gil said, "Come along, my dears." He crossed to the door, knocked, and opened it wide. "Good afternoon, Mr. Macri. I'm Gil Fulson."

"Come right in, young man."

Gil entered with Jack and Sally close behind.

Jack took just three steps across the thick carpeting,

92

when she took hold of his coat sleeve and gave it an anxious tug. "What?" he inquired in a whisper, turning to her.

Rising on tiptoe, she spoke softly into his ear. "That man sitting behind Giovanni Macri's desk," she told him, "isn't Giovanni Macri."

Chapter

12

The small bald man sitting behind the desk looked to be about seventy and was wearing a loose-fitting dark blue suit. "I been looking forward to this meeting, Mr. Fulson," he said, with a trace of an Italian accent. "Before we get going, though, introduce me to your colleagues, huh?"

"Actually, Giovanni, this young lady isn't—"

"Oh, yes, I am," said Sally angrily, in a nasal Eastern college voice. She let go of Jack, pushed by the director, and walked right up to the big desk. "You see, Gil didn't even want me to come, Giovanni, since he thinks I'm not actually right for the part of this commercial that his partner hired me for. He's anxious to drop me, but I've heard of your reputation for intelligent—"

"Lady, I don't want to get messed up in other people's squabbles."

"It's not a squabble." Sidearming aside several bottles of Macri Brothers wine that sat atop the desk, she rested her left buttock on it. "I was *hired* to star in this delightful commercial of yours, but now *he*—" She gestured accusingly at the perplexed Gil. "He, a man who actually boasts about winning an award for a commercial about a product that cleans toilet bowls— This man has the audacity to claim that I'm not *graceful.* He had the nerve to compare me to a hippo."

The spurious Macri said, "Lady, you go settle it outside my office, okay?"

"Look at me," she commanded, spreading her arms wide. "I'm graceful as hell—as any fool can plainly see."

Hunching in his swivel chair, the bald man frowned up at her. "I like them a little bit fatter myself," he said. "But then I'm not in the business of making TV commercials."

"No, you make this excellent wine." She grabbed a bottle of chablis, held it to the light and scanned the label. "You know wine, Giovanni, and I know what's graceful. It really wouldn't be smart to dump me now. I'd have to complain to my agents, to SAG, and—"

"Complain to who you want, lady, but get your butt off my desk."

Sally smiled sweetly at the imposter, slid her hand down the bottle until she was gripping the neck. "Right now I think you'd best take a nap." Without losing her smile, she brought the bottle down hard over his skull.

His eyes rolled, but he made a grab toward the drawer of the desk. "Bitch," he muttered.

She hit him harder, twice.

His eyes snapped shut, he groaned once. He slumped in the chair, unconscious.

Sally jumped off the desk, set the bottle aside, and yanked open the drawer the bald man had been reaching for. "Hey, a Charter Arms police bulldog thirty-eight special," she said, lifting out the gun. "I handled one of these when I did that 'Vice Cop' three seasons ago. Sure, I can use this to get him to talk when he comes around."

After blowing his nose, Gil cautiously inquired of Jack, "Do you have the remotest notion of what's going on?"

"Our host is an impostor."

The director sighed with relief. "Wonderful," he said. "For a while there I thought she'd bopped my client."

———

Sally led the way up to the second floor.

"This is getting awfully interesting," Gil confided to Jack in a careful whisper. "Interrogating that false Macri and then binding and gagging him. And afterward performing a similar act on that imitation receptionist. Very heady activities for a weary old—"

"Shush," advised Sally. She'd stopped in mid-hall and was pointing at a heavy wooden door with the barrel of the .38.

Jack moved close to her side. "Is this where they've got him?"

"Well, it's Uncle John's bedroom, which is where that down-and-out actor told us he's being questioned."

From inside the bedroom came a weak groan.

"Damn." Sally took an angry deep breath, knocked on the door with her free hand.

There was no response.

She knocked again, much harder.

"What the hell is it?" asked an annoyed voice.

"Listen, it's Nicki," she said, using the name of the young woman who'd been posing as the Macri Brothers' receptionist. "We got a big problem downstairs."

"Shit. Just a minute."

Thumping footsteps, then the door was unlocked and opened. The bear glowered out.

Jack kicked the door all the way open, causing the big man to go stumbling backward across the bedroom. He was the bear, all right—one of the two men they'd encountered in Connecticut at Buzz's house.

Sally leaped across the threshold, holding the gun in both hands. "Freeze," she instructed him.

On the spoolbed a thin old man in nothing but his underwear was sprawled. His hands were tied behind his back, there were three raw cigarette burns on his left arm. "Sally," he said in a faint voice. "I didn't tell them."

"Stay right there and don't move, you asshole," Sally told the big man. "I'm just about ticked off enough to shoot you for what you've done to Uncle John."

"Bullshit. A skimpy bimbo like you doesn't even know how to—"

She fired the .38. The slug dug into the wall less than three inches from the left side of his shaggy head. "That wasn't an accidental miss."

"Delightful," observed Gil from the doorway, chuckling.

Jack was untying the old man. "Easy now," he said.

Macri sat up once his hands were free. "Son of a bitch," he said in the direction of the bear. "We'll be taking care of you, boy."

Sally said over her shoulder, "Gil, get in here and tie this half-wit up. Good and tight."

The director entered and scanned the room. "Ah, those drape cords'll do just wonderfully," he said. "It's odd, isn't it? I've never been much into bondage before, but I'm finding all this marvelously exciting."

"Uncle John, that's Jack Deacon who's helping you," said Sally, keeping her eyes and the gun on the big man while Gil trussed him up. "A good friend of mine."

In a low voice the old man asked Jack, "Get me a bathrobe out of that big closet over there, please. I don't like standing around in my BVDs."

Crossing to the closet, Jack selected a robe and brought it back. "How many of these guys are there?"

"This bastard," said the old man while getting into the maroon robe, "that bastard who dressed up in my suit, a girl. Three other guys. They came in about eleven, with guns. Took over this building—they knew you were maybe going to be here today, Sally. And they brought me up here to ask about things." He took a few tentative steps. "Arm hurts like hell, but otherwise I'm okay."

"You have to get to a doctor," said Sally.

Macri started for the phone on the table next to his bed. "First I'll phone the cops to come and—"

"Not yet, please. We want to be away from here before they arrive."

"You in a lot of trouble, Sally?"

"No more than usual really." She let the gun drop to her side now that the big man was completely bound. "Did Shawn leave the trunks with you?"

"Just one. That's what this son of a bitch's been trying to get me to tell him about."

"Hell," the bear growled. "They're searching this dump. We'll find it without you, you old fart."

Macri gave a thin laugh. "They won't find it," he said, winking at Sally. "It's in the special place."

She smiled at him. "Of course. I should've thought of that."

———

The big brass lock on the door to the wine cellar had been broken. "They've already been down here," said Jack.

"Doesn't matter." With Sally's help Macri pushed the

heavy redwood door open. He entered and turned on the overhead lights. "Bastards."

Several of the wine bottles had been taken from their nests in the rows of wine racks and dropped on the stone floor.

Sally asked, "Do you know what Shawn did with the other trunks?"

"No, honey." The old man moved slowly among the rows toward the rear of the cellar. "I didn't even know there was more than one. Shawn asked me to keep it in a safe place for him and I did— Where is he anyway?"

Sally looked away, shaking her head slowly. "I'm not really sure."

"It's not drugs in the trunk, is it?"

"No, it's nothing like that, Uncle Jack. This is family property. Something that Shawn wants me to have."

Gil was inspecting some of the bottles in the racks. "I note he stores the product of rival vintners down here. Wise, considering the taste of some of the Macri—"

"How's that?" asked Macri from near the back wall.

"Merely commenting on what a delightful location this would make for future commercials, sir."

"That's right. You're the one who's supposed to be making my commercial today."

"We can postpone it until you're feeling—"

"We can start today, soon as the cops haul all those bastards away." He nodded to Jack. "Help me roll this barrel aside."

The two of them moved the ancient barrel a few feet to the left. There was nothing beneath it but cobblestone floor.

Crouching, the old man felt at the stones and then pressed two of them. "You used to like to hide down here when you were little, Sally."

"I remember, yes."

A section of the back wall made a rumbling noise

and swung open inward, revealing a small shadowy room beyond.

"Wonderful," exclaimed Gil. "Just like an old dark house movie."

"I keep the trunk in here." Macri entered the room and reached up to tug a light cord.

Sally went in next, hurrying to the large steamer trunk that was sitting in the middle of the otherwise empty room. The sides of the trunk were covered with a patchwork of long-ago travel stickers—Rome, Naples, Paris, Zurich, Lisbon. "Yes, this is one of them." The dusty trunk wasn't locked. She hefted the lid up and looked inside. "They're here, Jack."

"Superman, Action Comics, Batman."

Sally knelt beside the trunk, set her gun down, and very carefully explored the stacks of plastic-bagged comic books. "Yes, this is just about the whole DC part of the collection."

"That's what everybody's so damn excited about?" asked Macri, unbelieving. "Old funny books?"

"These are sort of special." Sally stood and faced him. "Very valuable."

"You going to take them with you now?" he asked her.

"I am, yes."

Jack said, "The only problem is how."

100

Chapter

13

There wasn't any shooting until just before they were about to get the comic books safely loaded and away from the winery.

The precipitating factor was the old decorative fish-pond near the gray stone garage building.

Jack and Sally, with some help from Gil, had transferred the plastic-bagged magazines from the trunk into cardboard Macri Bros. boxes—it took eight boxes to hold this batch. Giovanni Macri had also provided them with two hand trucks.

With Jack pushing one and Gil the other, they emerged from a side door of the main building and headed for the garages about a half-mile away.

Macri was leading the way. "This all looks perfectly natural," he said to Sally. "Just another shipment of wine going out."

"I doubt," murmured Gil, "anyone's ever ordered *eight* cartons of this swill at one time."

"How's that?"

Jack said, "We were saying that the fact you're in a bathrobe might strike some observers as odd."

"Naw, I'm a well-known eccentric."

"That's true." Sally was looking carefully around at the few visitors who were roaming the grounds of the winery.

The fish pond was about ten feet in diameter and contained more green scum than goldfish. Rising up out of its center was a very pudgy naked stone nymph who appeared to be trying to wrestle a dolphin to the mat.

Just as Jack was wheeling his loaded truck close by the pond, Sally exclaimed, "It *is* Walt!"

He looked back the way she was pointing.

A tall, lanky young man in his early thirties, with pale blond hair, wearing jeans and a denim jacket, was walking along a path about a quarter mile to their left. He hadn't spotted them as yet.

Jack's left wheel hit a large rock. The hand truck shook, stopped dead, then lurched in the direction of the pond.

The topmost carton of comic books jumped free, dropped to the edge of the water, and its top came flapping open. A half-dozen bagged comic books escaped, diving for the water.

"Good golly!" cried Sally.

Jack squatted, freeing the wheel. He gathered up the fallen box and reloaded it on top of the stack. "Murchison's spotted us. We've got to move."

Sally was kneeling at the pond edge, trying to reach the floating magazines. "Jack. That's *More Fun* number fifty-two and *More Fun* fifty-three. Worth, as a pair, at least six thousand dollars."

"Okay, okay." He waded into the water, scattering the curious goldfish who'd come swimming over to see what was drifting amid the green slime. He gathered up the bagged magazines and thrust them one by one under his arm. "There, I got all of—"

"No, look by your foot. That's *World's Finest* number two. Four hundred dollars."

"Oh, yeah, I see it."

Murchison was running toward them across the neat green lawn, right hand in his coat pocket as if he were clutching a gun.

Gil was already nearly to the open garage with his load. The Macri Brothers pickup truck they intended to use was sitting there half in shadow.

Jack, six wet plastic bags under one arm, started his truck rolling for the garage.

"Hold it right there, dude!" called Murchison.

"Enough of this." Uncle Giovanni reached into his robe pocket, tugged free a .45 automatic and fired twice.

Both shots hit the oncoming Murchison, one digging into each leg. He howled, both arms flapping, and fell flat out on the grass, as though someone had suddenly pulled out his feet from behind.

Sally had been reaching for the borrowed gun, which she had tucked in the waistband of her jeans. "I'm glad you shot him instead of me, Uncle John," she said, smiling and sighing. "It'll be a lot easier to explain to the police."

"I thought that robe felt heavy when I gave it to you." Jack started pushing his hand truck.

"I'm not going to comment on your clumsiness," said Sally, catching up with him.

"Don't," he warned.

━━━

They were back in their rented Isuzu again, having left the borrowed winery pickup at the Old Clarinda Inn. Two of the boxes of comic books were in the trunk of the car, the other six were stacked on the backseat.

Jack was driving. "They didn't suffer any water damage at all," he was assuring her.

Sally had the six magazines he'd rescued from the fish pond spread out on her lap. She'd carefully taken them out of their protective bags and was examining each one. Steepled over one thigh was the open price guide. "I guess the bags did protect them," she conceded. "But this *All-American Comics* number sixteen has an algae stain on its cover now."

Taking his eyes off the twilight highway for a few seconds, he glanced at the comic. "But that's not a fresh algae stain—you can tell."

"My father wouldn't have bought it if it had been defective, Jack."

"Jesus, a little splotch of green isn't going to—"

"Well, it might lower it's condition from mint to fine," she told him. "This particular issue contains the origin and first appearance of the Green Lantern—though this clunk on the cover doesn't look like any Green Lantern I ever saw before—and it goes for nearly six thousand in mint, but only three thousand in fine."

"*Only* three thousand?"

"I know even that's a lot of money for an old comic book, but six thousand is better."

"All right, I'll try not to drop any more of the damn things into bodies of water."

"You don't have to turn surly just because I make an—"

"Your ex-lover was shooting at us, Sal. We were trying to escape from an unknown number of hoods and heavies. So I had other things on my mind and I stumbled over—"

"Walt never got to draw his gun," she corrected.

104

"And . . . Wait now. Why don't we scrap that last bit of dialogue? I'm sorry I've been bitchy." Putting her hand on his nearest knee, she squeezed.

"Okay, all is forgiven."

Sally started slipping the comic books back into their clear plastic bags. "I think what we ought to do," she said, "is put this part of the collection in a safe place right away."

"A bank vault would be nice."

She snapped her fingers. "Allan's bank."

"Haven't heard of that one. Is it as big as Well's Fargo?"

"Allan Crandell is the vice-president of the Fisherman's Bank, the branch down near the Embarcadero."

"Local citizens fondly refer to it as just plain Allan's bank?"

"No, it's me who calls it that. I met Allan when I was doing a commercial in San Francisco three years ago."

"So far we haven't had much luck with your former suitors."

"He's reliable, stodgy even. We can trust Allan."

"Okay, do you want to drive on through to San Francisco tonight?

"No, going without sleep is starting to catch up on me. Let's stop at a motel in the next town. It ought to be Galinha."

"It is, I just saw a sign."

"I used to visit Galinha quite a lot, Shawn and I both did," she said, reaching around and very cautiously returning the comic books to their Macri Bros. box.

Galinha was a modest-sized town about ten miles north of San Francisco. Its central streets were tree-lined and just as they crossed its borders the street lights blossomed.

105

"Any suggestions about a motel?" he asked, slowing the car to conform to Galinha's posted speed limit.

"Other side of town I think. Something clean but unobtrusive." She was leaning forward in her seat, scanning the town. "It's still there—a restaurant Shawn and I used to like. I just noticed its sign down that side street, Grandmother Malley's. We used to go there for homemade pie and cocoa."

"We can drop by there later."

"Maybe," she said without much enthusiasm. "But I'm still uneasy about moving around openly in public."

Chapter

14

"Quaint," decided Sally.

"Quaint?" He nodded at the motel's flashing, multi-colored sign. "A ten-foot-tall cowboy playing a guitar, cactus letters spelling out Bashful Bob's Downhome Motor Inn?"

"Oh, the cowboy isn't more than six feet high," she said. "The important thing is it looks quiet and clean and not at all like the sort of place we'd be likely to spend the night."

"There is that. Okay, we'll try Bashful Bob." They'd been idling in front of the arched entryway of the motel grounds. Putting the car in gear, Jack drove the Isuzu in and stopped in a space in front of the office. The cartons of comic books bounced and thumped in the backseat.

The motor inn consisted of about two dozen separate adobe cottages circling a gravel courtyard. At the center of the courtyard stood a life-size or better plastic replica of a charging bull.

"Howdy now, folks." A big wide man in a black Western outfit had come trotting out of the motel office, spurs jingling. He wore a high-crown black Stetson and all his garments were trimmed with silver studs or fringe. Strapped low around his waist was a silver-studded gunbelt with two silver-studded holsters and a pair of silver-handled six-guns. "I'm Bashful Bob."

"You'd have to be." Jack eased out of the parked car. "We'd like a room."

"Cottage."

"A cottage."

"Each cottage has got its own bathroom, kitchen alcove, color television, and telephone," explained Bashful Bob. "The rate is thirty-five dollars per night, cheaper by the week. Or you might prefer the Honeymoon Suite—that's got a heart-shaped bathtub. Forty dollars per."

"The regular cottage'll be—"

"Hooboy! You planning to throw a party or what?" He was crouched, big hands resting on his knees, gazing into the back of their car. "That's more wine on the hoof than I've seen since—"

"My husband," explained Sally, sliding out of the car, "is a salesman for the Macri Brothers Winery. You've no doubt heard of them."

"Can't say I have, ma'am. Though I drink my share of wine." He whipped off his hat, gave her a polite bow. "You're one heck of a handsome lady, by the way."

"Thank you."

Jack took out his wallet. "We'll pay now, in cash."

"Heck, that ain't necessary, folks. I mean, just because I thought you was planning to throw a wild orgy

108

in my little motor inn, don't mean I won't accept your plastic."

"That's okay." Jack counted out three tens and a five and handed it over.

"Okay, thank you, Mr. . . ."

"Macri," supplied Sally. "He's the grandson of one of the owners."

"No kidding now, Mrs. Macri? And the old boy's got him out on the road schlepping vino, huh?"

Sally nodded, smiling at the big cowboy. "That's what the Macri family believes—you have to learn the business from the ground up."

"Well sir, I admire that philosophy. That's how I handled my career." He put his hat back on. "Maybe you don't recognize me out here in this light, but I'm Bashful Bob Webber."

"Really?" said Sally.

"I reckon you probably heard a lot of my country-and-western hits during your teenage years. That's when I was hot."

"No, I didn't," she admitted. "But then I attended school in Europe."

"Oh, heck, I was big in Europe. Especially West Germany."

"I went to school in Portugal."

Bashful Bob shook his head. "Nope, they never much took to me thereabouts."

Jack cleared his throat. "Shouldn't I sign in for us?"

"Sure enough, come on in and I'll have my wife get you the registration cards, Mr. Macri."

"Call me Jack."

"Okay, Jack. And let me ask you something—do you give out free samples at all?"

"Samples of what?"

109

Bashful Bob pointed a thumb at the stacked winery boxes. "Wine."

"Well, the company is a little—"

"Oh, Jack, don't be a grouch. We can give him one of the bottles that Gramps is sending to that awful restaurant owner in Fresno."

"You think we could, dear?"

"He'll never know." Smiling at the motel owner, she walked around the car and slid in behind the wheel. "Jack'll bring a bottle or two over to you as soon as we get settled in, Bob. Which cottage is ours?"

"Heck, I'm going to put you folks in the Honeymoon Suite—at no extra charge." He tipped his Stetson to her again. "That'll be cottage fourteen over yonder. Oh, and, ma'am, you got to park in back of the place, not in front."

Jack leaned in the open window and kissed her on the cheek. "See you soon, hon." He added in a whisper, "Where the hell do I get a bottle of wine?"

"Improvise," she advised him, smiling and starting the engine.

———

"Nobody will ever believe this," he commented.

"Oh, were you intending to blurt out everything about your personal life to the gang at Fagin's once you get home?"

He was standing just inside the door of their cottage, watching her sitting on the edge of the rustic wooden bed. "All I was commenting on was that this is our second or third night together. And we haven't even shaken hands."

"I don't recall I guaranteed you a roll in the hay when you signed on for this mission."

"Nor did I expect it," he told her. "Yet it seems odd

110

to me that you can think up so many excuses for getting me out of—"

"Why don't you stop nattering and get a bottle of wine for our host?"

"Let me bring in the luggage first."

"We don't need anything right now," said Sally. "Really, Jack, I'm worried he's going to get suspicious of us and phone the police or something."

"Motel owners never get suspicious, and they don't call the cops unless they find at least two corpses in one of their rooms. And even then maybe not."

"Well, humor me then."

"Okay, I'll drive back to the heart of town to a—"

"You can't drive, they'll notice you."

"I'm going to walk?"

"Aren't you the fellow who was bragging about how he ran over hill and dale in Brimstone, logging several miles a day?"

"I stated that I ran fairly often, but I wasn't bragging. Maybe the sedentary lumps you're used to keeping company with would boast if they ran more than fifteen yards without collapsing, but—"

"Hey, we're on the same side." She stood up, tapping a forefinger against the bronzed cowboy boot that sat on the rustic bedside table and served as an ashtray. "There were a couple of liquor stores only a few blocks from here."

"Yeah, I saw them when we were coming here." Turning, he reached for the doorknob.

"Not that way."

"Hum?"

"Bashful Bob and his wife'll spot you," she pointed out. "You'll have to go out the back way."

"There is no back way."

"Window in the bathroom." She gestured.

111

"I climb out a window, hike into town, and buy a bottle of Macri Brothers wine, huh?"

"Unless you want me to do it."

"No, nope, never. No, buying wine to con a washed-up hillbilly with is man's work." He tugged the bathroom door open, tromped across the cowhide rug, stepped into the heart-shaped tub, and tried to open the window.

It made several harsh, protesting squeaks.

"Not so loud, Jack," cautioned Sally from the doorway.

He nudged the center of the frame with the heel of his hand, succeeded in getting the window to creak open a few inches. Inserting both hands in the opening and gripping the lower frame, he shoved upward, grunting and muttering. Finally, the window opened fully. "It's raining now," he said, taking a look out into the night at their parked car and the surrounding shrubbery.

"That's not much." Sally had come into the bathroom and was standing in the tub next to him. "That's barely a drizzle."

"A professional weatherman would rate it as not far from a monsoon."

"C'mon, it's for a good cause." She gave him an encouraging pat on his backside.

Saying nothing, nodding grimly, Jack climbed out into the night and the rain.

━━━━ ∽ ━━━━

"The cash register is just about nearly empty," warned the thin young man behind the counter.

"Oh, so?" said Jack.

"And I'm neither Jerry or Glenn."

"Neither who?"

Nervously, hand shaking, the thin young man

pointed across the small liquor store at the front window. "As in Jerry and Glenn's First-Rate Liquor and Wine Shop."

"Well, I'm glad you told me that. Now if—"

"What I'm getting at is—it'd be foolish to stage a holdup here. There's nothing much in the till and I myself am not far from the poverty level."

Jack took a step back from the counter. "Do I look like a holdup man?"

"There's sure a wild and desperate look in your eyes, sir."

"That's because I *am* wild and desperate," he explained. "It has, though, nothing to do with my being a criminal. See, I've already been to three other liquor stores so far trying to buy a bottle of Macri Brothers wine and—"

"That stuff." The clerk laughed.

"That's pretty much the reaction I've been getting." He inched closer to the counter. "Would you maybe have—"

"I can give you a cheap Argentinian wine, sir, that's at least six times better than—"

"Has to be Macri. It's for a sentimental occasion, an anniversary actually."

"Boy, I don't know if I'd want to celebrate with anybody who drank Macri Brothers wine regularly."

"One bottle's all I need."

The young man looked at the surrounding shelves, thoughtfully. "You know, we might just have a couple of bottles at that. Jerry bought them by mistake a couple of Christmases ago— No, it was because the Macri salesman broke down and cried right here in the store. Jerry bought the stuff as a sort of Dickens gesture because of the season and all."

"Where is it?"

He tapped his cheekbone. "We put it up out of sight,

as I remember, so nobody'd see it and razz us," he answered. "Let me see if I can track it down." He reached for the rolling ladder.

"I'd appreciate that."

"Is this a lady you're getting this for?" He went climbing up the rungs.

"It is, yes."

"She must be pretty, huh?"

"She is."

"Even so you ought to really think about what you're doing, sir," he advised, moving himself along the high shelves. "Looks aren't everything in a good relationship. Taste counts for a lot more over the long— ha!"

"Found it?"

"No, but this is that Korean burgandy we bought once to help an orphanage. That means we're getting close." He moved along. "Eureka!"

"Macri Brothers?"

The clerk parted a row of bottles, reached into the gap. "I think I got her," he announced, chuckling. He brought out a bottle of white wine, blew off the patina of dust, and showed it to Jack. "Chablis okay?"

"Anything."

Cradling the bottle carefully, the thin young man descended. "Tell you what, sir, I'll let you have this for three-fifty. That's a buck off the price."

"Fine, thanks." Jack fished out his wallet from his hip pocket.

"How about a bottle of something decent for yourself?"

"No, this'll do."

"I hope you score, after all this."

The rain grew heavier and was falling with increased enthusiasm on the trudge home to Bashful Bob's.

114

Turning up the collar of his coat and hugging the packaged bottle to his chest, Jack started across the weedy field immediately behind their motel.

He bushed through the water-soaked high shrubbery behind their cottage and then stopped still.

Their car was gone.

Chapter

15

He didn't see the man with the gun until he'd stepped all the way out of the bathroom. "Where's Sally?" he asked.

It was the blond man and he was sitting in a rustic chair near the front door, pointing a .32 revolver at Jack. "I'd like you to tell me that, cobber."

"Why are you pretending to be Australian?"

"I *am* Australian, mate. Where's the bird?"

"I actually don't know." He was scanning the room for some clue, a note, something.

"Don't get the notion you'll be able to coldcock me with that bottle."

"We already did that bit once anyway." He set it on the bedside table, next to the bronzed cowboy boot. "Who are you working for?"

"Let me explain how this works, mate," said the blond man, swinging his gun six inches to the left and back. "The chap what has the gun is the chap what asks all the bloody questions."

"Way I figure it, you have to be tied in with Buzz, since Walt Murchison got to the winery ahead of you and I know he and Buzz aren't teamed up."

"It's the comic books I want to talk about."

"Hey, we never got them," Jack assured him. "They weren't at the winery."

"Sure, they were. I found that out by nosing around out there myself," he said, smiling thinly. "And with a bit of persistence, and some luck, I was able to trail you two here. Registering under the name Jack Macri wasn't all that bright."

"Look, we've reached an impasse," said Jack, feeling increasingly the damp of his rain-soaked clothes. "The fact is, she ran out on me. I have no more idea where the books are than you do. Sorry."

"I got a feeling you're going to remember, though." Slowly, smiling coldly, he rose from the chair.

A loud knocking started on the door. "Hope I'm not interrupting anything—but what about my free wine?"

The blond man was distracted by Bashful Bob's loud advent. He glanced for a few seconds toward the door.

Jack reached out, caught up the bronze boot and tossed it, hard, at the gunman. Then he threw himself flat out on the floor at the far side of the bed.

The boot sounded as though it hit him in the chest or the midsection. He made a pained gasping sound. Then his gun went off.

Next the door was smashed open.

"Drop it, friend," advised the voice of Bashful Bob.

"G'wan, you trying to scare me with those toy guns?"

Another shot, then two more.

Next came a bouncing thud and a groan, as the gunman collapsed onto the floor.

"Mr. and Mrs. Macri?"

"Yeah?" answered Jack from the floor.

"You folks okay?" inquired the motel owner. "I got a little suspicious when this gunsel come asking after you— eventually my missus suggested I mosey on over here."

Jack got to his feet, slowly and carefully. The blond man, he saw, was sprawled out on the Navajo rug and there was a bloody splotch growing on the left shoulder of his coat. Bashful Bob stood over him, a silver six-shooter in each hand.

"Thanks."

"Imagine this weasel hinting as how I wasn't handy with a shooting iron. I guess he never saw my three TV specials back in the sixties."

"Jesus, another blooming actor," muttered the fallen gunman.

The cowboy was glancing around, scowling. "Where's your missus, Jack?"

"She stepped out for a bit."

Bashful Bob noticed the wrapped bottle on the bedside table. "Well sir, ain't that nice. You didn't have to go and wrap it all up pretty."

"It's a standard publicity gesture my grandfather taught me."

"Well sir, I'd better drag this fellow over to the office and call the law." He holstered his guns, bent to retrieve the blond man's weapon. "I always hate having to explain the shootings around here to them. Ends up with them kidding me and calling me the Lone Ranger. What was this ruckus all about anyways?"

"It's sort of complex, but—"

The bedside phone rang.

Jack grabbed the receiver. "Sally?"

"No, this is Mrs. Webber."

"Oh."

"But I do have a call from your wife. Hang on, Mr. Macri."

118

Sally's first words were, "Where the heck have you been?"

"Where have *I* been?"

"Didn't you figure out my note?"

"I never saw a note."

"I left it right there on the darn—"

"Sally, we've had some trouble here and—"

"Are you all right, Jack?"

"More or less. Where are you?"

"I should've known you wouldn't be able to figure out anything subtle. I said I was going to recapture the past and I asked you to join me. Gee, I assumed you were bright enough to realize I meant I was coming to Grandmother Malley's and—"

"There was no note," he told her evenly. "Are you there now?"

"Of course, Jack, waiting for you. I've had two wedges of cherry pie already and—"

"Stay there. I'll join you shortly." He hung up, took hold of the bottle of Macri Brothers chablis, and walked out from behind the bed. "Compliments of the winery, Bob. I've got to go out for a bit to—"

"Oughtn't you to hang around until the cops arrive? I ain't exactly sure what all went on with—"

"My wife may still be in danger. Unless I can get to her right away, there's no telling."

"Well, okay." Bashful Bob accepted the wrapped bottle and tucked it under his left arm. "But you get back here soon as you can, Jack."

"You have my word." This time he left the cottage by way of the door.

***

"Frozen," he said.

"It isn't," she said.

"I've been living alone for several months. I know microwaved pie when I taste it."

119

Sally slumped slightly on her side of the pale green booth toward the rear of Grandma Malley's. "Maybe you're right," she said.

Putting down his fork beside his dish of blueberry pie, Jack said, "I want to get something settled."

"Go ahead."

"Was there really a note?"

"Of course there was." She sat up, stuck two fingers through the handle of her cocoa mug. "I left it for you on that little table next to the bed, with the heel of the cowboy boot weighting it down."

"Note wasn't there when I got back."

"Then you can assume Crocodile Dundee found it and took it."

"I never got around to searching him."

"You should've, since that's fundamental detective procedure."

"I didn't feel like performing fundamental detective procedures with Bashful Bob Webber looking on."

"Then we don't know who he is, or who hired him."

"Has to be in cahoots with Buzz." Jack picked up his fork, cut another bite of pie. "Otherwise he'd have been at the winery with Walt Murchison and his gang."

"He could've been a backup man."

"Not that far back. Nope, he's working with Buzz. And since we haven't seen Buzz yet, that has to mean he went to San Orlando first."

"He probably did, but he doesn't know who Sanlanda Sue is."

"You're sure?"

She took a slow sip of her cocoa. "Just about."

"Which means?"

"I've been thinking about this," she said. "There's a possibility—remote, however—that maybe I did tell Buzz a few things about my youthful escapades here in California."

120

"We'll find out for sure tomorrow."

Sally said, "There's another possibility that we haven't discussed."

"Which one?"

"It's something else I've been brooding about, Jack. Suppose—well, suppose this Australian is working for Shawn?"

"Your brother?"

"That Shawn, yes."

"He's dead."

"There's no proof of that. We only have Mutt's word, and you yourself told me he wasn't very reliable a person."

Jack watched her for a few silent seconds. "Okay, it's possible, Sally, that we'll find all of your father's missing collection," he said. "It's also possible that they'll net a couple million dollars. But that's all you can hope for out of this. You shouldn't be expecting that your brother is going to come back to life."

Very quietly, she began to cry. "Yes, you're probably right," she conceded. "It's only that—I'd like to see him again. I really sometimes miss him and . . . No, you're right. He's dead and I have to concentrate on other things."

He reached across, took her hand. "Coming to this place where you and Shawn used to hang out isn't going to cheer you up either."

"No, but I'm glad I came back." She took a tissue out of her purse. "Even if only to find out that their pies aren't homemade."

"They probably were back then," he said. "Why'd you leave the motel in the first place?"

"It was because I saw the blond man," she answered. "Right after you left I went up to the office to see if there was a coffee machine there. I happened to look across the street and there was his car. I didn't know it was his, but the way it was parked and the way the neon cowboy was flashing, I could see right into the driver's seat. I recognized him, but he didn't spot me. So I sneaked back, fast, to our cottage, wrote you that cryptic note, and drove over here." She wiped her nose. "I figured you'd come back through the bathroom window, see the note, figure it out, and come jogging over here."

"Our car's nearby?"

"Just around the corner, locked up tight."

"We'd better drive on to San Francisco tonight, deposit this part of the collection in your friend's bank as soon as it opens in the morning."

Sally poked her hand into her purse again. "Do you have any change?"

From his soggy coat pocket he took a handful of change and gave it to her. "Here. You going to make a call?"

"It might be a good idea to phone Uncle John Macri and find out what happened after the police arrived at the winery."

"Go ahead." He watched her walk gracefully to the phone booth near the entrance. Then he took out his sketchbook, which felt a bit damp, and opened it next to his pie dish. "Okay, let's see. Freddie's working as a waiter . . . he's baking a pie . . . he's using a recipe his cousin sent him . . . the pie comes out six feet wide . . . no, that's dumb. He's using his microwave to bake a pie . . . he's working at Mother Murchison's Cafe . . . customer complains about the pie . . . out comes Mother and it's a guy with a tattoo . . . God, that's awful. My sense of humor has vanished entirely."

"Nothing much." Sally returned and sat opposite him.

"Exactly." He shut the book and tucked it away. "My brain must be—"

"I meant from Uncle John," she said. "Walt and his associates refused to tell the police in Clarinda anything. They're in jail at the moment but will be getting out on bail eventually."

"What did Macri tell the police?"

"That they'd broken into his office and were after money."

"Nothing about us?"

"Not a word, no," Sally assured him. "So we ought to be safe for a while, what with Walt's gang and the blond man both locked up."

"There's still Buzz."

"Oh, yes, Buzz," she said. "I was trying to forget about him."

Chapter 16

Jack laughed again.

Sally was driving and didn't even look at him.

It was midday and they were nearly ninety miles down the coast from San Francisco, heading inland toward the mission town of San Orlando.

Shaking his head, Jack got out his sketchbook.

"Does that unseemly chortling you're doing," inquired Sally, "have something to do with the *Freddie Foible* ideas you're supposed to be working on?"

"Not exactly." He uncapped his pen.

"You could use a funny gag right about now. What you've come up with thus far has been pathetic."

"I'm thinking of giving up cartooning completely and switching to banking. I'd make a great vice-pres—"

"Are you going to continue to pick on me about Allan Crandall?"

"Nope. Sorry."

Sally said, "We've been on the road for two hours. Any halfway rational person would've dropped the topic a good eighty miles ago."

"Yes, I apologize. I've been behaving badly."

"After all, Allan simply exaggerated a little. It isn't as though he was an embezzler or anything. He just exaggerated his position at the Fisherman's Bank."

"Sure, that's no crime. I'd have done the same thing were I trying to woo a beautiful actress."

"He *is* head teller, after all, which isn't all that far from vice-president."

"It's admirable to have reached even that position by forty."

"He's not forty. He's prematurely gray."

"Lot of stress in banking."

"After all, Allan did introduce us to the actual vice-president. And everyone was very nice about storing the comic books."

"The VP hardly sneered when he realized what was in the boxes."

"Well, they had to inspect the contents. In case we were trying to put drugs or explosives in their vaults."

Nodding, Jack returned his attention to his book.

After about a mile of silent driving along the sunny road that wound through open fields, Sally spoke. "You're jealous. That's it. Because, gray hair or not, Allan is still a hunk."

"I'd rate him more a hunk-and-a-half. The guy must weigh—"

"He's tall and muscular, not overweight."

Jack recapped his pen, shut his sketchbook. "Let's switch to another category."

"All right. What did you think of the Pacific Ocean?"

"I've seen it before, remember?"

"Every time I drive along that stretch of coast highway—it's very exhilarating. Sometimes I think I'd like to live out here full time."

"You can."

"No, I have to stay in Connecticut to help run the Westport Artists School."

"The school's near collapse," he said. "And your partner may well be involved in a murder."

"That is, if he and Buzz are working together."

"They must be. That explains how Murchison got into this."

"Buzz could've hired him and then they had a falling-out."

"Maybe, but I'm dubious," said Jack. "If we can link Cobb with Mutt's murder, then he'll go to prison."

"That would mean the school'll collapse for certain."

"Could be it's overdue for that."

Sally said sadly, "My father, my brother—now the school, too."

He asked, "Do you enjoy running W.A.S.?"

"Not especially," she admitted. "But I owe it to my father to keep it going."

"That's not a very good reason for staying aboard a sinking ship."

"I can't abandon his school without— Hey, there's the turnoff for San Orlando." She guided the car over to the right lane, set the turn signal. "I think maybe I know one reason why your wife left you."

"Oh, so?"

"You're really not very good at humoring a woman," she told him.

———

"The town's changed some," observed Sally as they drove along Mission Street.

The mission itself stood on their left, made of adobe and dark wood and surrounded by a high, thick wall of

126

adobe. A huge, fluttering flock of white doves cut through the afternoon to roost in the branches of the willow trees showing above the wall. On their right rose a new, six-story hotel, all glass and metal, glittering in the sunlight. The sidewalks were dotted with tourists and locals.

"You remember where Sue's establishment is?"

"The other side of town." She slowed and stopped for a traffic light. "There's nothing out that way but farmland."

"This is the first time I've been in San Orlando," said Jack.

"Didn't you ever come here on a weekend or for a vacation?"

"We didn't vacation much. Although I did write a paper on the California missions for my fifth-grade civics class."

The signal changed and they continued on. "That Thai restaurant's new, so's the wine shop."

"Wonder if they stock Macri Brothers."

"I imagine most everyone does."

"Ha."

"That's right, you had a tough time buying a bottle last night." She turned onto a side street.

After several minutes of driving Sally began to frown. After a few more minutes, she said, "The outskirts of town have vanished."

"Obviously there's been a whole lot of building going on hereabouts. What's her address?"

"Twenty-sixteen Los Padres. That should be just ahead, except the farmland isn't there anymore."

The hillside up ahead was thick with brand-new two-bedroom houses on quarter-acre lots. Five Monterey pines had been planted near the entrance to the development.

"That was nineteen-ninety-five we just went by," he said. "Next block is it."

"But it isn't." She pulled the Isuzu up to the curb, parked, and turned off the engine. She got out, walked up onto the sidewalk. "Sue had a big, tottering three-story Victorian mansion right there." She raised her hand, pointed.

What rose up right there now was a cluster of six thin interlocked houses, each a different pastel shade. A sign on the narrow front lawn announced—*Camino Real Court/Condominiums Now Available/Inquire At Office.*

Jack got out of the car, stood looking at the fresh condos. "Maybe the condo office can tell us where Sue's gotten to."

"They may not even admit knowing her," said Sally forlornly.

———

The condominium office smelled of fresh paint and the chubby mustached man in the sea-blue blazer smelled of pine and leather. He rose up from behind his oak desk, smiling, extending an embossed business card at them. "Let me tell you right off, folks, that we only have two left," he said. "And you two look just like the sort of upwardly mobile couple who'd fit right in here at Camino Real Court."

"Oh, I just know we would, Mr. . . . ." Sally had become Southern again. She crossed the thick, sand-colored carpeting to the salesman and took his card. "Mr. Plumb. Isn't that cute little old name, Buford?"

Realizing he'd become Buford, Jack answered, "It is, pet."

Smiling sweetly, Sally perched on the edge of the big desk, crossing her legs. "I'll confide in you, Mr. Plumb—Gerard's your first name, is it?" she asked,

128

bringing the card up close to her eyes. "Do they call you Gerry?"

"Actually Ger."

"That's real cute, too. Mightn't I call you that, Ger?"

"Well, certainly, Mrs. . . ."

"Pond."

Plumb did a mild take. "Pond? What a coincidence . . . um, that is— Yes, of course, Mrs. Pond, you can call me Ger."

Winking broadly at Jack, she said, "Now what did I tell you, honeybun? There *is* a stigma attached here-abouts to your sweet old mama's name."

"There does seem to be." He moved closer to the desk.

"Even so, we've got to go ahead with our plan." Smiling, Sally took hold of Plumb's nearest arm. "I really and honestly think I can trust you, Ger."

"You most certainly can, ma'am."

"We came out here from Chattanooga to get reunited with Buford's sweet old mama. They've been estranged, on account of her unusual profession and all, for far too many years. But I recently told him, 'See here, honeybun, the old dear must have a stewpot of money and there's just no reason on this great green earth why she can't stake us to the down payment on a home. 'Fact, if we go to San Orlando we can kill two little old birds with one stone. We can make up with your long-lost mama and we can buy us one of those wonderful California condos we've always dreamed of.' But what a jolt we got when we came to his mama's address and found—"

"Mrs. Pond, I'm afraid I have some bad news for you both."

"Bad news?" said Jack.

"Oh, what is it, Ger?"

"If it's Susan Pond you're looking for—well, she died nearly a year ago."

Chapter

17

Plumb snapped another tissue from the redwood dispenser atop his desk. "There, there, Mrs. Pond," he said, handing it to her.

Sally added the tissue to the one balled up in her fist, dabbing sadly at her nose. "All this way, and we arrive too late."

Putting his arm around her shoulders, Jack made comforting noise. "You wouldn't know, Mr. Plumb, what happened to her belongings?"

The realtor was watching Sally sob into her hand. "You might inquire of that friend of hers."

"Who would that be?"

"She writes children's books now, though it's rumored she was once employed by your . . . Well, now. Her name is Katherine K. Lunsford. She does those Katrinka Belinka books that are so popular."

"Don't know them."

"If you had an eight-year-old, which we do, you'd know them. And have to buy every darned one as it comes out."

After delicately blowing her nose, Sally asked, "How can we locate this woman? If she was a dear friend of Buford's mother, he might enjoy talking with her."

Nodding, Plumb scribbled an address on one of his business cards and pressed it into her free hand. "She has a very impressive home over on Indio Lane. That's about—"

"I know where it is."

"You're familiar with our town? I had the impression you'd only just arrived in—"

"Goodness, I studied and just pored over maps of this dear little town before we ever left home, Ger." She left the desk and smoothed her skirt. "So I just feel like I know San Orlando's every nook and cranny."

Plumb said, "Should there be an inheritance—I can make you a very nice deal on one of our remaining condos."

Sally patted his cheek with the hand that held the soggy tissues. "Why, that's very sweet of you, Ger, but then I saw right off that you were a sweet little old dear." Smiling, she walked to the door. "Are you up to driving, Buford? Considering the real terrible shock you've just had."

Jack followed her to the doorway. "You'd best drive, dear," he said.

———————

As they walked up the wide, red-tile steps of the sprawling white stucco house Jack requested, "Let me pick my own name this time. No more Bufords."

"We're going to be ourselves this time," she reminded, reaching out to give the doorbell button a jab.

131

Chimes started to bong and echo inside Katherine K. Lunsford's home.

But nothing else happened.

Sally gave the bell another poke.

She was about to start knocking, when Jack caught her arm. "Quiet for a minute."

"What?"

"Listen."

After about ten seconds of listening, she asked him, "What am I supposed to be hearing?"

Jack made a hush motion with his right hand.

"Give me a hint at least," she whispered after another ten seconds.

"I thought I heard some noise in there. A thumping."

"Maybe we better try to get inside."

Jack grabbed hold of the brass doorknob, turned it. The door wasn't locked. Pushing it open, he crossed the threshold. "Hello? Mrs. Lunsford?"

From the rear of the big house sounded the hollow thumping.

"Down at the end of the hall," said Sally, entering the house and starting to push by him.

"Whoa," he suggested, catching hold of her elbow. "We'll approach with caution."

"C'mon, Jack, that's obviously the sound someone who's tied up in a closet makes." She pulled free, went running along the hallway.

He hurried after her.

"It's this one." Sally opened a dark-wood door. "Mrs. Lunsford?" Sally dropped to one knee and reached for the plump, red-haired woman who was sitting in the closet, bound and gagged.

The woman was about forty, dressed in tan jeans and a maroon silk blouse. Her forehead was red and bruised, and that was obviously what she'd been using to thump with.

132

Sally got the white tape off the woman's mouth with one quick, slightly shaky jerk. "Sorry."

The red-haired woman shook her head, spitting blood. "Thank you," she said in a stale, croaking voice.

Sally looked over her shoulder at Jack. "Give me your pocketknife."

"What would I be doing with a pocketknife?"

"All men carry one."

"You're thinking of Boy Scouts."

"In the kitchen," said the bound woman. "Last door on the right."

Jack went trotting into the kitchen, selected a carving knife from the rack over the butcher-block kitchen counter. "Are you Katherine Lunsford?" he asked as he squatted to cut at the ropes around her ankles.

"Yes, and you two are. . . ?"

"I'm Sally Westerland." She moved out of Jack's way.

"Oh," said Katherine Lunsford. "He mentioned you. You're Shawn Westerland's sister."

"Who mentioned her?" Jack cut away the last of the dirty ropes around her legs and went to work on those binding her wrists.

"The creep who dumped me in here."

"Blond guy, thickset and beefy?"

"That's the one."

"When was he here?" Jack unwound the last coil from around her wrists and started massaging them.

"It was—Lord, a day ago at least. I think I've lost track of time." She struggled to rise. "Before we do anything else—help me get to the bathroom."

Reaching into the closet, he put an arm under her arm and around her back and helped her get, very unsteadily, to her feet. "Where is it?"

"Closest one is right across the hall." She held tightly to him. "Christ, I'm woozy."

"We'd better," said Sally, "phone somebody for you."

133

"I'll give you the number of my doctor in a minute," she said. "But no cops. The reason for that is—well, I haven't always been Katherine K. Lunsford." With Jack's help she crossed the hall.

"We know about that." Sally opened the door for her. "Do you have a trunk my brother left with Susan Pond?"

"I had it stored," she answered. "But, honey—I'm afraid I had to tell him where it was."

The antique shop was on a quiet side street. It was wedged between a defunct boutique and a completely empty store that had a hand-lettered sign announcing *Mothers' Rummage Sale Soon!* taped to the inside of its window. The antique shop's one small display window contained a jumble of objects, including three japanned boxes, a small windup phonograph, a gilded Venus, a brass ibis, a wicker basket filled with dusty peacock feathers, an empty hourglass, a stuffed owl, a nest of crystal eggs, and a plumed hat.

Just to the left of the gargoyle doorknob was a pushpinned index card explaining *Away in Europe.*

"The comics will be long gone." Jack took hold of the knob.

"But Buzz may've left clues," said Sally. "We have to start somewhere."

The door didn't open. "Locked, and Mrs. Lunsford says she gave Buzz the only key she had to her friend's shop."

"It's still difficult for me to imagine Buzz threatening to burn that woman with a cigarette," said Sally.

"Was he especially gentle with you?"

"Not exactly, but he never tried anything like that. Besides, he told me he'd given up smoking six months ago."

134

"Let's," suggested Jack, "see if there's a back way."

A bit listlessly she accompanied him around the brownstone side of the building and into the weedy lot at its rear. "I keep trying to look on the bright side," she said. "We do, after all, have roughly one third of the comics. But still— Damn it, I hate to think that Buzz has a third, too."

"This is odd." He was crouching, studying the handle of the back door to the shop.

"What?"

"This door's been jimmied," Jack pointed out. "And somebody also took the trouble to disable the rather primitive alarm system." He pointed upward.

"Buzz must have done that."

Jack straightened. "Why would he? He had the key." He turned the door handle and eased the door open.

Nothing but silence and shadows on the other side.

"Musty," observed Sally, brushing at the tip of her nose.

"The dust of time." Jack entered the wood-planked hall. "There are the stairs leading to the storeroom she told us about."

Sally shut the door quietly behind them. "If Buzz didn't break in, who was it then?"

"Somebody from the Murchison spinoff group," he answered, starting up the stairs. "Or a completely unrelated burglar who's after stuffed owls."

"I'm getting increasingly ticked off." She followed him up the creaky wooden steps. "More and more people are trying to swipe *my* comics."

"Treasure hunts can get that way."

The lights, such as they were, were on in the upstairs storeroom. That meant a nineteen-twenties floorlamp with a parchment shade and an imitation-Tiffany hanging from the ceiling. The clutter was impressive, a blownup version of the jumble in the antique shop's

135

front window. A bentwood rocker loaded with Spanish shawls sat next to the bottom half of a dented suit of armor, a guitar rested against a child-size pink marble Venus with a clock in its stomach, the bust of a Civil War general—most likely Robert E. Lee—lay in a copper bathtub it shared with at least a half-dozen feather boas, a stuffed owl was perched atop a banjo case, three pairs of boots stood in line in front of—

"It's dad's trunk!" exclaimed Sally, pushing by a claw-footed hat rack, stepping over a fallen mannequin, and halting in front of a trunk that looked quite similar to the one they'd found in Giovanni Macri's wine cellar.

Jack, almost knocking over a tall stack of dusty hat boxes, joined her. "Easy now."

"Maybe he didn't take them after all." Anxiously, she bent and got hold of the trunk lid. She lifted it open wide. "Oh, my god."

Inside the trunk there were no comic books. Only the dead body of Buzz Wisebecker.

Chapter

18

The park was small and the redwood bench they were sharing was ringed by willows and high grass.

Sally was sitting at one end of the bench, hugging herself and leaning forward.

Jack sat in the middle, watching her.

"Is it cold here?" she asked finally.

"Not especially." They were in a patch of bright sunlight.

"God, I feel so awfully cold. No, I don't want anybody to touch me."

He'd started to edge closer to her. "Okay."

After a moment she said, "This is very rough."

"I know."

"Until a few days ago I thought I loved him. Then I realized he'd only been after the two million dollars worth of comics and I switched to hating him. And now we find him dead and . . . Shit, I don't know how I feel." Bending farther, she started to cry.

Jack ignored her earlier warning and moved next to her. He put a hand on her bent back and massaged gently.

Sally sniffled. "It's very strange, looking down at the corpse of someone you've been sleeping with."

High up in the clear afternoon sky an invisible jet was inscribing a neat white line that pointed southward.

"We have a couple of obvious courses," Jack said, continuing to stroke her slim back. "We can quit right now and go to the police."

"Whatever we do, we can't just leave him in the trunk."

"No."

"But— Damn it, who killed Buzz?"

"He looks to have been dead for a day or so," said Jack. "I'd guess that Murchison or somebody working with him trailed Buzz here to San Orlando, followed him when he visited Mrs. Lunsford. Then, once he led them to this batch of comic books, they killed him."

"And then they came up to Clarinda and the winery?"

"Probably. I searched Buzz. He didn't have the Tijuana Bible, which probably means somebody took it off him."

"Even with the map, how'd they know to come directly to Uncle John's winery?"

"Buzz may've known and they may've persuaded him to tell them."

Sally said, "All this time, just about the whole damn time we've been in California—Buzz has been dead."

"Yes."

"I was cursing him and he was stuffed in—"

"Sally, listen." Jack lifted his palm from her back.

"Death doesn't really change much when it comes to somebody's character. Buzz was a son of a bitch before he ever met you, he remained one, and even now he's still one."

She made an angry, gasping noise and stood up. She raised her hand, as though to slap him. "You're a son of a bitch, too," she accused, crying, sniffling. "I loved him once."

"Bullshit." He stood up and faced her.

"You've been sounding sympathetic and now you turn into a shit."

"I've given you all the sympathy I think the situation calls for," he told her. "Beyond that, Sally, I'd just be humoring you. There's no reason for that."

"You're being heartless."

"Okay, let's go to the cops. The station is three blocks from here, near the mission," he said. "We'll explain the whole setup, tell them where to find Buzz and that we suspect Walt Murchison may be the one who knifed him."

She wiped a knuckle under her nose. "And what about the rest of my comic books?"

He shrugged. "We'll probably have to forget about them," he said. "Unless the cops can track them down. The batch in San Francisco is worth a lot and you'll have to settle for that."

She inhaled, exhaled, nostrils fluttering. She clenched her fists. "No, goddamn it. Nobody's going to get away with stealing my comics from me."

"So?"

"I don't much like you at the moment."

"I figured."

"But, all right. What's an alternate plan?"

"We try to pick up the trail of this batch of magazines."

"How exactly?"

139

"Whoever it was who took them may not want to haul them all over before cashing in."

"You mean they'll try to sell them right away?"

"Yep, and I noticed a comics shop while we were driving over to the antique store," he said. "A long shot, but let's see if anybody's tried to unload any of them yet."

"And what about Buzz?"

"As soon as we're ready to leave town, we can call the police and inform them—anonymously."

She looked down at the ground for a few seconds. "Okay," she said. "It's not great, but that's what we'll do."

Chapter

19

There were magazine racks covering three of the walls of Funny Paper Smith's Comic Shop. The racks were filled with current issues of comic books, fanzines, graphic novels, and collections of newspaper-strip reprints. In the center of the room were four long narrow tables holding cardboard boxes displaying back issues.

Two plump teenage boys were scanning the racks at the right of the store, a short middle-aged man with a fuzzy mustache was leafing through a reprint book of *Li'l Abner,* and the young clerk was sitting behind the glass counter with both plump elbows on it. He was reading a tabloid newspaper and ignoring a slice of pizza cooling on a paper plate next to one of his elbows.

He glanced up when Jack and Sally entered, smiled, and then returned to his reading.

"We'll pretend to browse first," Jack told her quietly.

She took a slow look around the store. "They still print all kinds of comics."

"They do."

"Which ones does Goldberg draw?"

He answered, "*Death Squad Two, Kalifornia Killbillies,* and he just took over *Mutant Mercenaries.*"

"Which one would you recommend?"

"*Killbillies.*"

"He really draws something with a title like that for a living?"

"Everybody can't draw *Freddie Foible.*" With his hand resting lightly on the small of her back, he escorted her over to the "K" section of the wall racks.

"*Katy Keene* looks more my sort of thing."

"There it is—next to *Kamikaze Kids.*"

"It costs a dollar seventy-five?"

Grinning, Jack plucked a copy and placed it in her hand. "A slice of Grandmother Malley's pie goes for two-fifty."

"And it's probably more stimulating to the brain."

"Excuse me," said one of the plump young customers. He was wearing pretattered jeans, a large, wide-shouldered jacket, and a blank T-shirt. "But are you two into *Killbillies*?"

"No." Sally shook her head as he approached them.

"I'm in the process," explained Jack, "of converting her."

"That's actually a bad book to get into the Maximus Gestalt with," the young man advised them. "You really want to introduce her with something like *Flaming Death* or *Commander Blood.* But *Kalifornia Killbillies* is really lame."

142

"I'm actually," said Sally, pressing the magazine to her breasts, "more interested in the drawing."

Both teenagers laughed.

The second one added himself to the group. "Goldberg is bogus."

"Bogus?" asked Jack, starting to scowl.

"Unless, you know, you like artists who do nothing but swipe from Frank Miller and Howard Chaykin. Goldberg hasn't done anything but—"

"Goldberg doesn't swipe," cut in Jack, voice rising. "Or if he does, he doesn't swipe from his inferiors. He's intelligent enough to swipe from illustrators like Wyeth, Lyendecker, Stoops, and—"

"Yeah, but there's also the problem of his flawed sequential sense," said the first plump youth.

"That's right," said the second plump youth, shaking his head pityingly. "Goldberg has no sequential sense at all."

Jack said, "That's absolutely a half-wit judgment. Goldberg can take the average dim-witted, insipid Maximus script and turn it into a—"

"Jack, dear," said Sally, taking a portion of his jacket sleeve between her thumb and forefinger and yanking vigorously, "we have to buy our comics and then rush home to fix Aunt Beth's dinner. Nurse is going home early today, as you well know."

"But if you guys aren't even capable of seeing that Goldberg's approach to staging a story is infinitely more sophisticated than that of a Chaykin or even a Sienkewicz then you've got your tastebuds up your—"

"Anyone who seriously considers a typical Goldberg page," said the first plump young man, "has to see that he doesn't know a damn thing about panelology or flow."

"Flow? Flow isn't important unless you know how to make pictures, sonny. And what—"

"Jack. We have to get going."

He looked at her, shook his head once from side to side. "You're right, yes." He grinned thinly at the pair of plump youths. "Very stimulating chatting with you, fellows."

"You aren't all that old yet," said the first one. "There's still time for you to educate yourself."

"Thanks, that gives me something to live for." He allowed Sally to tug him up to the cash register.

"*Kalifornia Killbillies,* huh?" said the plump clerk as he slipped the magazine into a white plastic bag that had the slogan *Get With The Maximus Gestalt!* printed in red on its face. "That'll be a dollar seventy-five."

Sally took two dollar bills from her purse. "Perhaps you can help us," she said, smiling her best hopeful smile. "My twin sister has been bedridden ever since a terrible horseback riding accident during her senior year in college. Her chief interest in life is collecting old—that is, Golden Age—comic books. Because of a sizable legacy from an uncle who invented several basic automobile parts, she's able to collect on a grand scale."

"We don't stock much Golden Age, ma'am."

"Well, I've just heard a rumor that a fairly large collection has turned up right here in San Orlando," she said as she handed him the money. "We were really hoping to find out who—"

"How about that?" He tapped the edge of his paper plate. "Just yesterday."

"Just yesterday what?" asked Jack.

"Guy came in and tried to sell us—oh, it must've been a hundred Golden Age comics. All in fine to mint, but we don't have the budget, or the clients, for that sort of stuff."

144

"What sort of titles?" asked Jack.

"There was some prime stuff—*Human Torch* number one, *Sub-Mariner* number one, a run of early *Marvel Mystery,* and, one I'd never seen before, *Captain America* number one."

"The Marvel part of the collection," murmured Sally. "Who was offering them? Perhaps we can contact him directly."

"I didn't get his name, since we don't deal in Golden Age on that scale. I mean, *Cap* number one, you're talking anywhere from five to ten thousand. It was beautiful, too. Jack Kirby art."

"What'd he look like?" inquired Sally. "Slight, dapper man of about sixty with a gray crewcut?" she said, describing Jarrett Cobb.

He shook his head. "This guy was—oh, in his late twenties, I'd guess. About five-ten, and on the thin side with blond hair. It was about the same shade as yours, ma'am, matter of fact."

Sally touched Jack's arm. "That almost sounds like it could be Shawn."

Chapter

20

~~~~~~~~~~~~~~~~~~~~~~~~

"Eat your pie," Jack advised.

"It's nowhere near as good as Grandmother Malley's."

"A lot better than Fagin's."

"I wouldn't know."

They were at a small round table in a small restaurant a block from the comics shop. The afternoon outside was just beginning to fade.

"Checking out every comics shop in this part of the state," said Jack, pausing to chew a bite of his blackberry pie, "isn't the best idea. According to the clerk at Funny Paper Smith's, there isn't another one in San Orlando and those in surrounding towns aren't big enough to buy a big collection. So I think they'll try to sell them at the comic convention he told us about. The one coming up day after tomorrow in Yatesville."

"But if it's Shawn that's—"

"I don't think it is."

"The way he described him, I—"

"Whoever brought in that sampling of the collection has to be the same person who killed Buzz. Or at least he's working for the killer."

Putting both hands around her coffee mug, she leaned forward. "I know that, and I don't believe Shawn could kill people," she said. "Still, it sounded so much like him, right down to the hair. Both my brother and I have blond hair of the same exact—"

"So do millions of others, especially in Southern California. In Sweden they've got a whole country full of—"

"Okay, all right." She leaned back in her chair. "Yes, it does seem probable that they'll want to hit this upcoming convention. Since that'll give them access to forty or fifty dealers from all over, plus some gung-ho collectors. But that's two days away."

"We still may be able to beat them to the Hootman ranch."

Sally rubbed her fingertips across her forehead. "That's right, the third trunk of comics must be there," she said in a tired voice. "Because maybe Buzz didn't know about Hootman, because maybe I never mentioned it. And maybe they never got him to tell them and maybe they haven't figured out that part of the map in the Tijuana Bible."

He caught one of her hands, held onto it. "You're sounding groggy."

"I'm in grand shape," she insisted, pulling her hand free. "The movie ranch is about a hundred and seventy-five miles south of here, near a little town named Winship. We should be able to drive there in no more than five hours."

"Why don't you try to call him first?"

She shook her head. "Dan Hootman's not listed with information," she said. "I thought I told you that. I tried to track him down by phone the same time I was hunting for Sanlanda Sue's number."

"Let's hope that doesn't mean he's dead and gone, too."

"Let's hope the ranch is still there." Pushing back in the chair, she stood. "I'm ready to go."

———

"Did I doze off?" asked Sally.

"Yep."

"Good thing I'm not driving."

It was, according to the dash clock, 8:14. They were moving along a patch of highway between towns, dark fields stretching away on each side and in the distance the tiny lights of a scatter of houses.

Sally yawned. "That's twice, isn't it, since we left San Orlando?"

"There times."

"We were having a conversation about— Yes, I remember. I was pointing out how compulsive I've become lately." She pressed her back against the seat, thrust her legs out, and pressed her feet against the floorboards. She yawned once again. "There we were in a town with a famous mission, one that tourists flock to see. And we didn't even go inside to take a look."

"We're not tourists." Jack yawned.

"Yes, but that doesn't mean we have to shun interesting places and historic landmarks."

"It does if we want to beat the competition to the rest of the comics."

"I'm not going to bring this up again, but doesn't it seem like an incredible coincidence to you that the very man who tried to sell what we're just about certain are my comic books was an exact double of my brother?" She sank lower in her seat. "It goes beyond the laws of probability."

"All the guy in the store said was thin and blond," he reminded, taking a deep breath. "Thirty-seven percent of all males in California fit that description."

She glanced over at him. "Are you aware that your eyelids keep drooping and nearly shutting?"

"I am. I'm fighting it."

"We'd best stop for coffee in the next town."

"We stopped for coffee in the last town."

"You're right, we did. It didn't help much."

"Suppose," he suggested, "we stop at a motel and sleep for, say, five hours."

"Six," she said. "That way we can get a good, adequate rest and still be back on the road no later than four twenty-one A.M."

"An excellent time for driving."

"Exactly, because there's very little traffic on the road."

"The sun doesn't get in your eyes."

"There are no school buses to hog the highway."

"What's this sign say? Willisville six miles," Jack said. "We can stop in Willisville."

"It's the home of McNider's Cider."

"My mother used to put little jugs of that in my lunch box."

"What sort of picture did you have on your lunch box?"

"No picture. It was a no frills, generic lunch box."

"I had Batman."

"Upper-class kids could afford luxuries like that."

"Sure, and a maid to carry it to school for me. Were you smart in school?"

"Average."

"Could you draw even when you were small?"

"Yes, better than I do now. Is that a gigantic apple coming up on our right?"

"It is. Made out of tin, I think, and they have to re-paint it that bright red every summer. It's twenty feet high."

The huge metal apple sat at the side of the road on the fringes of Willisville. Ground-level floodlights illuminated it and the large white letters proclaiming— *Home of World-Famous McNider Cider.*

After they'd driven about two-and-a-half blocks into the town, Jack said, "That's where we ought to stay. The Adam and Eve Motor Lodge."

"Agreed," said Sally. "And when you register, make sure they don't give us twin beds."

Chapter

21

It was the first time in a while he'd awakened beside a naked woman. Eyes still shut, Jack lay close to Sally and savored the experience. Her bare legs were warm and smooth alongside his, her right hip was pressed pleasantly against his left buttock.

The motel bedroom seemed awfully bright, though.

Opening his eyes, he saw that Sally was sitting up in bed, two pillows behind her back, reading. The bedside lamp was on and the fat paperback she was studying was the comic-book price guide.

"Do you realize what that run of *Marvel Mystery Comics* they highjacked from us is worth?" she inquired. "At least seven thousand five hundred dollars. And that's not including number one, which goes for around twenty-five thousand all by itself."

Jack said, "Isn't this an interesting coincidence? I was

just lying here beside you wondering about those very funny books."

"You sound miffed."

"Why ever would I be miffed?" He started to sit up.

Sally tossed the book aside, caught his arm. "I thought you were asleep and I got to wondering about my missing magazines." Slipping an arm around him, she kissed him.

He took hold of her, hugged her hard for a full minute, saying nothing.

Sally said finally, "It's, by the way, six A.M."

"Weren't we going to get back on the road by four A.M.?"

"But you were sleeping and I decided a couple hours wouldn't matter. You look very innocent, and cute, asleep."

"So I've been told."

"By your wife?"

"Don't you think I have any friends of my own?"

"*Freddie Foible*, 1975."

"No, that punchline's a lot older than that." He kissed her a few more times. Then, reluctantly, he let go and got out of bed. "I'll get dressed."

"That's interesting," she told him, watching him collect his clothes from a chair. "I wouldn't have guessed you were that orderly. Folding each garment neatly."

"A middle-aged trait," he explained, getting his shorts on. "In my youth I tossed them hither and yon."

"Too bad I'm encountering you in the winter of your life." Smiling, she left the bed and made her way to the bathroom. "I love you," she called through the open doorway. "Did I mention that last night."

"No."

"I meant to."

152

They located the Hootman ranch a little after eight in the morning. It was exactly where it was supposed to be in the hills at the edge of the town of Winship.

There was a large log ranch house, a stable and corral, a block of false-front 1880s Old West buildings, and a huge barn scattered across the six-plus acres. It was framed by woodlands.

"Barn's had some trouble," noticed Jack as he drove through the open gate in the rail fence.

"Pretty bad fire."

About a third of the red barn had burned down. Its back walls were jagged and black, fallen timbers stuck up through the gaps.

A large black mutt was sprawled in front of the door to the house. He got casually to his feet and then started barking ferociously.

Jack parked the Isuzu next to a weather-beaten buckboard. "Now we have to find out if any of Hootman's kin are still around."

"Dan could be alive." Sally got out of the car. "Let's try to be optimistic."

Growling and barking, the big dog came charging at her.

"Halt right there," Jack advised as he came out of the car.

Swerving, the dog ran toward him. Five feet away, it halted and stood snarling. Then its tail began wagging.

"Nice boy," Jack said tentatively.

The dog jumped up, put its forepaws on his middle, and tried to reach up to lick his face.

Jack patted its bumpy head. "At least the watchdog likes us."

"Who the fuck are you?" The door of the house

had opened and a Chinese in his late twenties was glaring out at them. He wore jeans and a faded gray sweatshirt.

Sally, smiling, approached him. "We're trying to locate Dan Hootman."

The young man grinned and stepped out into the bright morning. "Are you people affiliated with the entertainment world in any way?"

"I'm an actress."

"Do you have any influence in the music business?"

"Some."

Reaching back into the house, he brought out an acoustic guitar. "I've been trying to break into the music business for three solid years."

"I'm not exactly an expert on rock music."

"I don't play that shit," the Chinese explained. "I'm a rural blues singer."

"Really?"

"You know, in the tradition of Blind Lemon Jefferson, Big Bill Broonzy, Robert Johnson, Son House, and—"

"What about Dan Hootman?" Fending off the friendly dog, Jack worked his way over to the house.

"Oh, the old fart died two years ago. Are you in show business, too?"

"No, I'm a cartoonist."

"That's okay. I'm going to need somebody to draw the covers of my record albums," he said, hanging the guitar around his neck. "Let me try something out on you. Which name sounds better? Lightnin' Foo or Muddy Foo."

"I think maybe the Foo part detracts in both cases," answered Jack.

"Yeah, that's the trouble with being a Chinese blues singer named Benson Foo."

Sally told him, "We've come a considerable way, Benson, to find out if—"

154

"You can call me Lightnin'."

"Fine. The point is, though, what can you tell us about Dan Hootman?"

"He croaked."

"Ben, what are you doing out there? Not inflicting your music on some poor innocent wayfarers?" A small, thin young woman, about twenty-one years old and no more than ninety pounds, appeared in the doorway. She had on jeans and a faded yellow sweatshirt.

"I haven't played one single tune, Nyoka."

"You've got to watch him and keep a tight rein on him," the young woman explained. "Otherwise it's 'Whiskey Headed Woman Blues' and 'Electric Chair Blues' and lord knows what else until your ears are fit to drop off in the—Sally!"

Sally had been studying the young woman intently. "You're Peggy Hootman, Dan's granddaughter."

"I am, sure. Except my name's Nyoka Amberson. Nyoka because it looks good on my paintings and Amberson because I was dumb enough to marry a geek named Bill Amberson three years ago for a few months." She patted Benson's shoulder. "I was pretty young and drunk back then. But Ben's helped me a lot this past year and I'm sober and a little wiser. I turn out about two paintings a month now and last year I actually sold three."

"You were only so big when I used to . . . But you're still only so big now, as a matter of fact." Sally moved ahead and she and Nyoka hugged each other.

Ben nodded at Jack. "She your lady?"

Jack said, "I think maybe she is."

"She's the kind of woman, to quote Lightnin' Hopkins, that'd make a monkey hug a hound."

"Is that good?"

"Sure. Same as being the kind of woman who'd make a one-eyed man go blind."

Jack said, "The reason we're here, Ben, is—"

"Call me Muddy."

"I thought it was Lightnin'."

"I like to try them both out, get a feel for which sounds better."

"Well, Muddy, we're looking for something that Sally's brother may have left with Nyoka's grandfather."

Nyoka let go of Sally and took a step back. "That's right, Sally, Shawn was here about two or three years ago if not before. Grandpa did mention Shawn was leaving something for him to look after."

"A trunk?"

"Not sure, since I never saw what it was. I was pretty heavy into liquor and drugs around that time."

"Dumb," observed Ben, the fingers of his left hand forming a chord on the guitar strings.

Sally asked, "Where would it be, whatever it was?"

"Not in the house," said Nyoka.

"Shit," said Ben, frowning at her.

"You think so?" she asked.

"What's the problem?" asked Jack.

The young woman sighed. "Grandpa kept a lot of stuff, especially from his movie days," she said. "He probably put what Shawn gave him in with that stuff."

"And that stuff is kept where?" asked Sally.

"That's the trouble," Nyoka pointed to the left. "He kept it all over in the barn—and in the fire last fall we lost near half of that."

Chapter

22

Sally coughed again, brushing back her hair with a sooty hand. "I just found one of Dan's scrapbooks, Nyoka," she called. "Don't you think you ought to keep that in the house?"

"I suppose." Nyoka and Ben were rummaging on the far side of what was left of the barn.

Sally was on the opposite side, Jack in the middle.

Everything that had been piled there, and that included packing crates, cardboard boxes, suitcases, trunks, saddles, guns, costumes, books, and hardware was crowded on the floor of the extant part of the old barn. A good half of that was now under fallen, charred timbers and heaps of ashes.

"They sure haven't been treating this place like a shrine," muttered Jack as he tried to tug aside a burned plank.

"Jack!"

He turned, looking toward Sally. "What?"

"Underneath these water-soaked cowboy outfits," she said excitedly. She was shoving chaps, shirts, and sombreros off something. "Yes, it's the trunk."

He worked his way over to her. "You sure?"

"Of course, look at the travel stickers."

By the time he reached her, she had all the costumes off the trunk and was trying to lift the lid. "I'll help," he offered, taking hold of one side and tugging.

The comic books were inside, stacked neatly, each protected by a clear plastic bag.

"*Police Comics* number one—at least eight hundred dollars, *Military Comics* number one—a thousand, *Amazing-Man Comics* number five—two thousand dollars," Sally recited as she went through the contents of her father's trunk. "This is the remaining third of the collection, Jack. And I'm pretty sure it's all here."

"Yeah, it seems to be."

She glanced up at him. "Something the matter?"

"I don't know," he told her. "It's only that this was almost too easy."

They came down the stone steps of the Winship post office hand in hand. "Good thing we have that cash Wally loaned you," Sally said. "It certainly cost us a lot to mail those comic books up to Allan's bank in San Francisco."

"Four crates sent express mail can cost a lot, yes."

"Want to stop for lunch before we head for Yatesville?"

"Okay, but I want to talk about something."

"Last night? I haven't had any second thoughts if that's what—"

"No, about the comic books."

158

"Now who's being crass and commercial?"

They were passing the town square. Jack led her over to a wooden bench near a pedestal holding a bronze statue of a World War I soldier. "We now have approximately two-thirds of the magazines," he said, sitting beside her.

"You've been acting spooky ever since we found the second batch in the Hootman barn. What is it?"

"We think it's Jarrett Cobb who's behind this," he said. "He was able to find out the other two locations, but this one is a little trickier. Whitehat City has eluded him."

"Yes, so?"

"He knows we're hunting for the magazines, too. He probably is even aware that we got the batch at the winery."

"He probably is," she agreed.

"His batch is worth around half a million at least," continued Jack. "Not a bad take, but the whole collection will bring three or four times that."

"Jarrett wants it all, we already agreed on that."

"Rather than come down this way, rather than even tailing us—he could just wait."

"You can't be sure he's not hunting," she pointed out. "For all we know he's got a crew of goons in Winship this very minute and in six other towns in the vicinity. Maybe he's also got a crew checking the registration cards at every motel from San Orlando to L.A."

"Possibly," acknowledged Jack. "But it's also possible that he assumed we'd do a better job of finding this third part of the collection than he could."

"Then he was right."

"He might figure that all he has to do is grab us and take the comics from us."

"But we don't have them. Everything is safely in Allan's vaults or en route there."

159

"Cobb has no way of knowing that. He may think we're still hauling them around with us."

"But how can he try to grab us, Jack, since he doesn't even know where we are?"

"Now, no. But he's got a good idea of where we'll be tomorrow."

She sat up straighter. "The comics convention in Yatesville," she said. "You're suggesting that they deliberately showed some of the comics in San Orlando, deliberately asked where they could sell them. Cobb *wants* us to follow him."

"I'm suggesting that he could have something like that in mind, yeah."

"Darn," she said, exasperated. "You're in love with me, too."

"Obviously."

"That's making you sentimental," she said. "You don't want me to get hurt."

"Cobb, or whoever is behind this, has already killed two people," he said. "I don't want you to get killed, Sally. And, if possible, I'd like to stay above ground myself."

"I appreciate that, Jack, but—"

"We can quit right now. Drive up to San Francisco and sell the magazines we already have. We'll net over a million dollars."

She stood up. "I mean to get back every comic book in the collection, all of them."

He sat watching her for a few silent seconds. "All right then, we'll go after the rest," he said, rising. "But we're going to have to be extremely careful."

"I already have that on my list of things to do," she assured him.

160

Chapter

23

He was reaching for the phone when the door of their hotel room opened. "Anything?" asked Jack, getting up off the bed.

Shutting the door with her backside, Sally carried over the three newspapers to dump them where he'd been sitting. Kneeling beside the bed, she turned to an inside page of one of the papers. "There's nothing at all in the *Yatesville Observer-Democrat*," she said, "but the *Santa Barbara Press-Guardian* has it. The headline is *Body Found In San Orlando Antique Shop*. It goes on to say that the local police, acting on an anonymous tip—that's us—found the body of Bruce Wisebecker, age thirty-eight—he always told me he was thirty-five—in a steamer trunk in the store's attic. He died of multiple stab wounds to the chest and there was evidence he'd been tortured before . . . well, no need to go into that."

"Any suspects? Anything we don't know?"

"An unnamed witness supposedly saw a black van parked behind the shop on the day they think Buzz was killed. That's about all. They're trying to locate the shop owner, wherever she's vacationing in Europe." Sally rose and brushed off her knees. "Nobody saw us, the police haven't connected Katherine Lunsford with the trunk, they don't even know why Buzz—who's described as a 'public relations executive with a prominent Connecticut organization'—was in town. In other words, everything seems to be a mystery to the police."

"Unless they're not confiding everything to the press." Jack picked up the Gideon Bible he'd been using as a clipboard and tapped the sheet of hotel stationery. "Here's what I've been finding out. Firstly, Jarrett Cobb isn't registered here at the Van Buren Hotel—not under that name anyway."

"But he is staying here, Jack." Sally settled into the flowered armchair beneath the painting of the New England covered bridge. "He's calling himself Jules Coopersmith."

"How'd you learn that?"

"Well, while I was down in the lobby buying the local papers—*Freddie Foible* doesn't run in any of them, by the way—"

"We've got the *Los Angeles Times* and the *San Diego Union,* so we—"

"Just thought you'd like to know, since the comic strip is your only source of livelihood." She paused to shrug, then continued. "I had a conversation with the desk clerk."

"That chinless redheaded guy who was ogling you while we registered?"

162

"He's got a chin of sorts. His name is Leroy and I explained to him that I'm a reporter with *Los Angeles* magazine, here to cover the comics convention," she said. "I described Jarrett and told Leroy that he was a famous cartoonist from the east I was anxious to interview. But that Jarrett shunned publicity and usually traveled incognito, emerging only for a brief appearance at the convention. Leroy recognized him from my description. Jules Coopersmith, Suite thirteen-oh-one. That's just two floors above us." She pointed a forefinger at the ceiling.

"What about the comic books?"

Sally smiled. "Mr. Coopersmith had four large cardboard boxes with his luggage."

"Bingo," said Jack, but quietly.

"You don't sound exactly enthusiastic."

"Those boxes could just be the cheese in the trap."

"Well, certainly. Keep in mind, however, that we're smarter than he is," she reminded. "What else have you come up with?"

"The kid back at Funny Paper Smith's gave me the name of the guy who's putting on the convention here tomorrow. A local dealer named Phil Zeeburg."

"Have you talked to him?"

"I phoned his shop. They say he's already checked into the hotel here, getting ready for the con. That's what you call them—cons, not conventions," he told her. "I was about to try his room when you reappeared."

"We have to approach him carefully," she said. "Since I can't prove that I own those comic books. When you ask if he's heard anything of a big collection of Golden Age comics or if anyone's planning to try to sell such a collection at his con—you can't sound like a comic-book bandit."

163

"I was planning to be discreet, but maybe you ought to phone Zeeburg."

"No, you can be as glib as I can."

He sat on the wide bed, dialed the hotel switchboard. "All the time I've lived in Connecticut, I've never seen a covered bridge or . . . Phil Zeeburg's room, please."

The phone rang seven times before a youthful voice answered. "What?"

"I'd like to speak with Phil Zeeburg."

"So would about seven dozen other assholes. Who are you?"

"I'm the one who's not an asshole. My name's Jack Deacon."

"Hold on." The receiver dropped on to something hard.

Sally raised an eyebrow. "Why the asshole remark?"

"Ah, youth," he said.

"Is this a joke or what?" inquired a thin nasal voice. "Is this some archrival of mine attempting a feeble scam?"

"This is Jack Deacon. I'd like—"

"You're claiming to be the famous cartoonist, Jack Deacon?"

"I'm a cartoonist. As far as famous goes—"

"You were written up in *Cartoonist PROfiles* last year. That Jack Deacon?"

"Sure, that's me. But—"

"*Freddie Foible* is my favorite strip. The ones you ghost are the best of the best—especially that wild, cynical cockroach stuff. You bring joy to my otherwise drab life and lighten the burden placed on my frail back by crazed comics fans and three violent and vicious ex-wives. Can you appear as a guest at my con tomorrow? I'm assuming you're in the vicinity and not in the wilds of Connecticut."

164

"I'm right here in the Van Buren."

"Good. I'll set you up at a table amidst the dealers. You can sign autographs, shake hands. Did you bring anything to sell? *Freddie* paperbacks? Originals? Sketches?"

"Nope, but I'd like to talk to you about why we're here."

"We? Jesus, you're not with your wife? What a horrible way to travel this great land of ours."

"I don't have a wife anymore."

"This is starting to sound better. Somebody else's wife you're with?"

"A friend. Can we get together for a—"

"I'm in thirteen-twenty. Come on up—is now okay?"

"About ten minutes." He hung up. "Zeeburg claims to be a fan of mine."

"That's great. You ought to be able to recruit him to our side."

"We can both do that. C'mon, he's—"

"I'm feeling sort of tacky. I want to take a shower and then rest." Getting up, she came over to him. "When you finish with Zeeburg, we can go out to dinner. Do you like Mexican food?"

"Within reason."

"I saw a nice-looking place while we were hunting for the hotel." She kissed him.

Jack held onto her for a while. Finally he pulled back, saying, "Imagine having to come all the way to Yatesville to find fame."

———

"He'll regret this later," prophesied Zeeburg to Jack. "You're going to regret this later, Lex."

"He doesn't even draw for comic books," replied Lex from the bedroom of the hotel suite.

"I'm giving you merely five more seconds, putz—

then you don't get to meet Jack Deacon and shake his hand."

No response came through the half-open doorway, only the sound of gunfire and automobile tires from the murmuring television set.

"Proving you can't beat heredity," explained Zeeburg, who was a small, wiry man of forty. He wore black jeans, a black leather jacket, and black running shoes. "My son's mother—the first of my trio of wretched wives, now much in demand for road companies of *Macbeth*—the lad's mom was sullen, vapid, and mean-minded. The poor kid's inherited all those traits of hers and more, but not a smidgen of my wisdom, wit, and grace."

Jack said, "Let me explain why—"

The phone rang in the bedroom.

It rang six times.

Then Zeeburg said, "Answer the thing, putz."

"What?" said the unseen teenager in answering. "It's Rudy, Pops."

"I'll call him back."

"He says he's got to have an extra table tomorrow."

"All the tables are sold."

"He's starting to whine and snivel."

"Okay, I'll see what I can do. I'll call him." Zeeburg gestured toward the flowered armchair. "Sit. Want a warm root beer? A slice of cold pizza?"

"Neither, thanks." Jack sat on the edge of the chair, found himself staring at a painting of a New England covered bridge. "I'm out here with Sally Westerland."

"A gorgeous actress," said Zeeburg. "I fondly remember her from a perfume commercial two years ago. She was wearing nothing but black lace lingerie and walking through the windswept ruins of an Aztec temple. 'I may be crazed, but I must have Revulsion. The essence of madness by Maurice Wepman.' Very

166

classy and—which you are no doubt aware of—she looks splendid in black lace. But I interrupted."

"Sally and I are on the trail of a very valuable collection of Golden Age comic books that were stolen from her—"

"She collects comics, too? Marvelous." With bouncy steps, Zeeburg walked to the flowered sofa and sat. "There are women in this world who look great in black lace undies. There are others who collect old comics. But when you find one who does both, hold onto her."

"The comics belonged to her father."

"An excellent artist."

"We suspect that part of the collection, which was stolen, is here. It may be put on sale at your con."

Zeeburg bounced twice on the sofa. "The Coopersmith collection. Is that what you're alluding to?"

"Yep, except Coopersmith is really Jarrett Cobb."

"A second-rate artist. Make that third-rate," said Zeeburg. "He stole the comics from Sally Westerland?"

"It's more complicated than that, but Cobb's the one who has them now."

"Can't she just go ask him to give them back to her?"

Jack told him, "Two people have been killed already over these things. Cobb's not going to give them up."

"Fans," said the convention organizer, "they'll stop at nothing."

"How did you hear about the magazines?"

"Coopersmith, alias Cobb, phoned me at my shop late yesterday. He mentioned some of the stuff he had and asked if I'd be interested," recounted Zeeburg. "I was interested, yeah, but we're talking about around three hundred thousand for what he seems to have. Once I had dough like that, but three shrews later I don't."

167

"So you suggested he attend the convention?"

"I told him to take a table, but Cobb said he'd prefer simply to attend and see if any of the dealers or customers were interested in making an offer."

"You haven't actually seen any of the comics?"

"Not yet, Jack. But I'm going to very soon."

"How's that?"

Zeeburg bounced to his feet. "Because you and I are going to steal them back for Sally."

Chapter

24

"You look terrific," Zeeburg assured him.

"Red isn't my color." Jack tugged at the waiter's jacket he'd donned, trying to get it to fit a bit less snugly.

"Trust me, you make a very convincing waiter." Zeeburg, who was decked out as a bellboy in a gold jacket and silky black trousers, took another look toward the door of his suite. "I think it has something to do with the menial look you get in your eyes."

"Working with Wally and teaming with Sally causes that." Jack drummed his fingers on the silver cover of one of the dishes on his borrowed waiter's cart. "You have considerable clout with this hotel."

"Yatesville isn't a major convention town. So certain people on the staff appreciate me—I'm the closest thing to Diamond Jim they've got." He buffed the gold buttons on his jacket. "Besides which, I know which of the lads on the staff are running hookers into the Van Buren. It's to their advantage to do me favors."

"Your clothes fit better than mine."

"That's due to my compact build." Zeeburg moved nearer to the door. "The best thing about this caper is that Cobb isn't likely to report it to the law or even complain to the hotel."

"It seems unlikely that he'd risk having a conversation with the cops." Jack checked his wristwatch. "I'd still like to phone Sally to explain—"

"No phone communications. The bimbo on the switchboard this shift is no partisan to my cause. Further, due to a misinterpreted pat on the ass delivered during an elevator ride earlier in the year, she considers me several rungs lower on the social ladder than Jack the Ripper."

"Okay, but—"

Someone knocked on the door. Three short, two long, one short.

"Cobb's left his room. That's one of the few things Lex shines at," said Zeeburg, grinning. "He's really very handy in any enterprise that smacks of larceny."

"You've done things like this before?"

Zeeburg opened the door a few inches. "This is not the time or place for true confessions." He stepped carefully into the hotel corridor.

There was no sign of his son.

The wheels on the white-cloth-covered serving cart squeaked, and in pushing it into the hallway Jack bumped the doorjamb and set the dishware to rattling.

Whistling softly, Zeeburg went striding along the hall. The passkey he'd acquired a few moments earlier was clutched in his right hand.

They moved briskly along, with Jack having a little

trouble keeping the cart on a straight course. Around a bend was room 1301.

Halting, Zeeburg looked carefully up and down the corridor. "Not a soul in sight." He tapped politely on the door.

No response came.

He knocked again.

"Okay, let's break and enter. Cobb and his roomie are definitely out." He thrust the passkey into the lock, turned it, and opened the door.

Cobb's suite smelled of cigarette smoke and musky aftershave. Zeeburg walked rapidly across the living room. "Mr. Coopersmith, sir, are you here?"

Jack pushed in his cart and shut the door. "Covered bridge," he observed, noting the painting above the flowered sofa.

"Holy moley!" exclaimed Zeeburg from the bedroom.

Jack hurried in there. "The boxes."

There were four large cardboard boxes lined up against one wall. Zeeburg was squatting before one, which he'd opened and was rummaging, carefully, through. "Look at this. *Sub-Mariner* number one, *All-Winners* number one, *Daring* number seven," he recited. "Would that I were truly the Raffles of comicdom. I'd hold onto these gems and thus ensure myself a worry-free old age. Ah, *USA* number one. Wolverton is in this one and I've never seen what he did." He lifted the comic book out of the box and started to slide it from its clear plastic bag.

"No time," reminded Jack.

"Yes, right you are. Excuse my fannish impulse. We have to scram."

Jack said, "You can keep the magazine."

"Keep it? My lad, it's worth at least a thousand bucks."

171

"Consider it your fee for helping out."

"Done." Zeeburg undid two buttons of his shirt, slipped the comic book inside, and rebuttoned. "My humble thanks to you and Missy Westerland, bwana." Bending, he lifted up the box.

Jack hefted another one and followed him back into the living room.

Lifting up the skirt of the long white tablecloth, Zeeburg placed the box of comic books on the sheet of plywood he'd arranged on the cart earlier. "All four of them'll fit under here."

Jack set his box next to it and returned to the bedroom for another. "Let's hope Cobb doesn't come back before we—"

"Relax, we've only been looting his quarters for about five minutes."

"Seems longer."

Zeeburg took a look in the third box before he stowed it on the cart. "*Captain America* number one on top, plus a *Miss Fury*."

Jack fetched the final box and set it on the makeshift platform. "That's it." He arranged the tablecloth so it masked all the boxes.

Zeeburg was already at the door of Cobb's suite. He inched it open and scanned the hallway. "Oops, a hooker en route to her john," he reported quietly. "We'll wait." He eased the door shut, whistled silently, studied the ceiling. "Okay, it's clear," he said after taking a second look.

Jack pushed the heavy cart out of the suite. "That was fairly easy."

"Crime often is," said Zeeburg.

———

Getting the boxes down to the hotel garage by way of a service elevator and loaded into the trunk of the Isuzu took nearly fifteen minutes. Changing back into

172

his own clothes and bidding Zeeburg farewell consumed another ten.

By the time he got back to their room, Jack had been gone over an hour-and-a-half. "We can take off right away," he announced, after letting himself in. "I got them."

She didn't answer.

He heard water running behind the closed bathroom door.

"Sally?" He knocked on the door.

Still no answer.

He opened the door and went in.

The faucet over the sink was gushing hot water, the small white room was steamy, the mirror was fogged, and on the yellow tiles of the floor lay Sally's hairbrush.

He took a deep breath, pulled aside the shower curtain. The stall was empty.

Turning off the water in the sink, he returned to the other room.

He noticed now that the Gideon Bible had fallen to the floor next to their bed. Nothing else was out of place.

He circled the room, slowly, twice. There was no note, no clue as to where Sally had gone.

Probably just out for a newspaper, he told himself.

He sat in the flowered armchair.

She'd have left a note.

Maybe she had become tired of waiting and just gone out to get something to eat.

She'd have left a note.

Okay, then perhaps she'd gone looking for him. But he was just at Zeeburg's. His son had been there, watching television again. He'd have mentioned if Sally'd been there asking for him.

He was a surly kid, though. He might not have both-
ered to mention it.

How about Sally just got tired of you and took off?

Nope, it was too soon for that. It had taken his wife
several years to work up to fleeing.

Sally could simply be down in the lobby, buying as-
pirin or something like that.

What he'd do was leave a note, in an obvious spot,
and then go down to see if she—

The phone rang.

He hopped free of the chair, dived for the bedside
phone, and had the receiver to his ear before the third
ring.

"Sally, where the—"

"Mr. Deacon, is it?" It was a quiet, almost lazy, male
voice.

"Yeah?"

"We find ourselves in a somewhat ironic situation,
sir. While you were robbing my suite, I was kidnapping
dear Sally."

"Cobb," said Jack. "Listen, you'd better let her go
right—"

"Please, please, Mr. Deacon. Calm is what's called for,
not empty threats," said Jarrett Cobb. "I have no real
desire to harm Sally. After all, I've known her since she
was a sweet, golden-haired child. And much less of a
pain in the ass she was in those days, I assure you."

"Are you suggesting some kind of deal?"

"Exactly," said Cobb. "Sally has admitted to me, after
a little persuasion, that you still have all the comic
books in your possession."

Getting control of his anger, Jack lied, "That's right,
yes."

"The deal I have in mind is simple. The entire collection, including those you just stole from me, in exchange for Sally."

"Okay. How do we go about it?"

"You're being, I must say, quite agreeable."

"Sally's more important to me than a bunch of old magazines."

"Very touching," drawled Cobb.

"But before we go any further, Cobb, I have to talk to her."

"That would be most difficult."

"I saw what you did to Buzz," he told him evenly. "You're going to have to convince me Sally is alive or it's no deal."

"Yes, I suppose yours is a sensible request," said Cobb, thoughtfully. "Please hold the line."

Jack noticed he was breathing through his mouth, rapidly and shallowly. He concentrated on stopping that.

"Jack? I'm sorry—they conned me out of the room." It was Sally, her voice weak and sad. "I had to tell them you had all the magazines. There was—"

"That ought to be enough to convince you, Mr. Deacon," cut in Cobb.

"Yeah, okay. How do we work this?"

"Bring all the comics to the old Glennoffer Mansion," instructed Cobb. "Be there in one hour. Obviously confide in no one, come alone, and don't bring any police. If you don't cooperate in every way—we'll kill Sally. Is that understood, sir?"

"Where's the Glennoffer Mansion?"

"Twenty-one-sixty Hillside Drive. One hour." Cobb hung up.

"Shit," said Jack.

Chapter

25

He was still driving up the winding hill road when the lightning and thunder started. The overgrown fields turned a sudden glittering, electric blue and the ground seemed to shake.

Jack rolled up his window. "Appropriate weather."

Sitting beside him in the passenger seat were two cardboard boxes filled with comic books. There were seven more boxes stacked on the backseat.

Lightning struck again, illuminating a string of run-down tract houses on his right. He was able to read the number on the rusted roadside mailbox of the last one in the row. It was 1870 Hillside.

Rain began. A fast-falling, warm rain that splattered the car and the slanting roadway.

The Glennoffer Mansion sat on three weedy wooded acres, surrounded by a high stone wall. Only half of its

176

wrought-iron gate was still there. Hanging askew from that was a faded, weathered wooden sign warning *No Trespassing*.

He slowed the car, turned off the road and onto the rutted circular driveway. There was light showing at a few of the shuttered lower windows. The house was a huge Victorian.

Lightning crackled again.

The abandoned mansion briefly turned a pale, shimmering blue and all its intricately carved gingerbread stood out. Then darkness closed in again.

Driving up close to the old house, Jack parked near the ramshackle five-car garage. He sat there for a moment, the rain hitting the car, and studied the front of the house. The light was showing in what was either a parlor or living room. It had the pale, flickering quality of lantern light, or a television.

Lightning flashed once more and showed Jack a lean blond young man. He wore a yellow slicker and held a large black umbrella not over his bare head but over the .38 revolver in his right hand. He was a few feet in front of the car, smiling at Jack and beckoning to him with his gun hand. The blue light faded and Jack saw only a dark blur in the hard rain.

He opened his door and put out one foot, as though he were testing the water in a pool.

"Come on out, jerkoff," suggested the man with the gun.

"You ought to wear a hat. Rain's going to take all the curl out of your—"

"Out, then up on the porch."

"I brought all the comic books. Don't you want me to start carrying them in?"

"I'll handle that, you just hustle your ass up onto the porch."

Once they were on the wide wooden porch and protected by its roof, the blond young man tossed his umbrella aside and proceeded to frisk Jack. "No weapons. A nice tight butt."

"Don't let Cobb hear you. He's liable to get awfully jealous."

"Inside." He prodded him in the back with the barrel of the gun.

Jack opened the oaken door, stepped across into the hall. It was dimly lit, full of deep shadows. There was a heavy smell of damp and decay.

A small gray man in slacks and blazer was leaning in the parlor doorway. He had a snub-nosed .32 revolver dangling in his hand. "In here in the parlor, if you please, Mr. Deacon," he requested.

Jack went into the parlor. "Damn it," he said. Sally was on a tattered loveseat, a white handkerchief serving as a bandage around her lower right arm. "What the hell did they—"

"It's okay, Jack," she said. "Nothing too serious. I didn't want to tell them we still had all the comic books, but—"

"That's okay." He sat beside her, put an arm carefully around her shoulders. "I brought them all over."

"I hate to give them up."

"We don't have a choice." He got up and helped her to rise.

There was no rug on the hardwood floor. It was streaked with thick dust and some of the boards were scarred with cigarette burns and others had initials and short profanities gouged in them. There were scattered animal droppings, the remains of old meals eaten by squatters, even a few discarded contraceptives.

Sally said, "We filled our part of the bargain, Jarrett."

"You'll have to wait, I'm afraid, until my young associate brings all the books inside," said Cobb from the wide doorway.

"He's the one who took the samples to Funny Paper Smith's," Sally told Jack. "The one who fits, somewhat, the description of Shawn. That's how they conned me out of our room, by claiming Shawn wanted to see me."

"We'll go over the whole thing later," said Jack. "Cobb, I brought all the magazines. Now we're going to leave."

"Eventually, in due time."

"It has to be within an hour," Jack said. "I didn't quite live up to our agreement."

"Really now?"

"I told someone where I was going. If I don't contact him—in person—within an hour—and with Sally—then he calls the police."

"Oh, an hour should give us plenty of time."

The blond young man came puffing into the hallway, lugging a cardboard box. "Jesus, these fuckers are heavy."

"Put the box in the parlor," Cobb instructed.

Legs slightly bowed, the blond young man dropped the box in front of the dead fireplace. "You want me to haul every damn one of those boxes in here?"

"Yes, and as swiftly as you can," urged Cobb. "It turns out, thanks to Mr. Deacon, that we're working under a very tight deadline."

"Raining like hell out there now."

"Nevertheless, it must be done."

"I'll be happy," offered Jack, "to give him a hand."

"That won't be necessary." Cobb made a get-going gesture with his left hand.

Grumbling, the young man headed back out into the storm.

Sally kicked at the box. "Jarrett, the ransom is here— or it will be as soon as your toady gets around to carrying it in," she said. "You can let us go now."

179

"Open the box, please," he ordered her.

"It's taped shut."

"You'll have to risk your fingernails, my dear. Hurry now."

Kneeling, Sally started tugging at the masking tape. "I wish I hadn't done such a thorough job of packing these."

Jack asked him, "What about the Westport Artists School, Cobb?"

"Defunct for all practical purposes," he replied. "With the two million or so I'll realize from this foolish collection of Sally's father, I'll be able to live relatively well in some warm and obscure foreign country. With any luck I'll never see snow again."

"There," said Sally, "it's open."

"Very slowly and innocently, dear, lift out the top magazine and hold it up."

She complied. "It's *Captain America* number four."

"Set it on the floor and show me the next one in the stack."

"Here, *Mystic Comics* number six."

"They're all Golden Age, Cobb," said Jack. "I wouldn't try a bluff with Sally's life at—"

"Show me the next comic book, dear."

"Um . . . *The Adventures of Superman* number four thirty-three."

"And the date on that one?"

"I don't see one, but I'm sure this is a very old—"

"It's printed in that box in the upper-left-hand corner. Read it."

"October 1987."

Cobb's gun swung over to point at Jack. "Really, Mr. Deacon, did you actually think I'd be fooled by a couple of valuable magazines atop a stack of garbage?"

"I underestimated you."

"You can stand, Sally," said Cobb. "This was hardly a

180

brilliant ruse, Mr. Deacon, and I don't see what you hoped to gain from it."

"Well, in the first place I couldn't have gotten inside this place without what looked like a carload of old and valuable comic books," Jack explained, inching closer to Sally. "And hauling these boxes in here and looking through them would buy us time. And, of course, if you had been fooled by what was on top and let us go, all the better. Actually, I figured from the start you'd kill us both once you got the real stuff, anyhow."

"What did you need time for?"

"For the police to get here, surround the house, and quietly sneak inside."

Scowling, Cobb said, "I warned you not to notify the police."

"You did, but I went ahead and ignored you."

"That's right, Mr. Cobb. He did." In the doorway appeared a tall, wide uniformed policeman with his gun drawn.

Chapter

26

Two-and-a-half weeks later Jack was sitting on a warm stretch of Southern California beach. The early-afternoon sky was only moderately hazy and the sun was bright. Up above a group of sea gulls was gliding and stunting. A few of them came diving down, cawing, to go skimming along the ocean surface.

Jack watched them through his dark glasses. "Life can be like that," he said to himself, "nothing but an endless pursuit of garbage."

"You don't tan well," said Sally, approaching him from behind.

"Sure, I do. Bronze is the ideal shade that sunbathers strive for. And that's exactly the shade I've turned in the time we've been renting the beach house."

Sally had just come walking across the sand from the deck of the glass-and-redwood house some two hundred feet away. "I was just talking to Mr. Krigbaum of Krigbaum, Reisberson, and O'Brien on the phone," she said. "Of all our lawyers, I like him the best."

Jack moved to the side of his crimson beach towel. "What'd he tell you?"

"Well, we're going to have to stick around in California to testify at the various trials." She sat down beside him, sharing the big towel. She was wearing white shorts and a sea-blue T-shirt. "But he doesn't think anybody is going to charge us with anything."

"That's good news."

"Perhaps by the time all the legal business is done with, I'll understand what actually went on."

"Seems to me that Buzz and Cobb started out as partners," he said. "When Buzz got his hands on the Tijuana Bible and your brother's map, he decided to go out on his own—especially since you'd already confided enough of your past to him to enable him to figure out the code names Shawn had used."

"I still can't believe I told him all that much."

"When you informed him that Mutt was in the vicinity and intending to make contact with you, Buzz alerted Cobb," Jack went on. "It occurred to them that Mutt might think you were still residing at the same old place—my current place—and they dispatched thugs to both locations to waylay him. The guys who went to the old location were the ones who got—"

"Yes, you explained that to me before," she cut in. "Do you think, now that everything is over and done, that Buzz actually took part in the torture and killing of poor Mutt."

"Hard to call." Jack shrugged.

"He did slip out after Mutt's call, but . . ." She shook her head. "Well, we do know for certain that he decided, once he saw the Tijuana Bible, to go into business for himself."

183

"Yep, but Cobb tumbled fairly soon that Buzz was double-crossing him and he put Walt Murchison and assorted louts on his tail," continued Jack. "They caught up with Buzz in San Orlando, just as he located one of the trunks. They questioned him, killed him, and took the map. Next they rushed up to the winery in Sonoma County. Got there ahead of us and in time to put a fake Uncle Giovanni in place. After we incapacitated most of them, Cobb and his blond buddy came West to take over."

"And that blond man who tailed us to Bashful Bob's motel had been Buzz's partner, right?"

"Yeah, somebody he'd alerted to keep an eye on you, in case you got free of your cellar and decided to head for California."

Sally smiled. "Well, I'm glad that fate tossed you and me together."

"I collaborated with fate some. Since I wanted to get tossed together with you," he admitted. "Ever since I saw you standing in my closet, I knew—"

"That's not a very romantic way to meet. We'll have to come up with something better for your biographers."

He asked, "Did you call Allan's bank?"

"Yes, and those checks cleared. We now have six hundred thousand dollars," she said. "Not bad for selling a little more than a fourth of the collection to those two San Francisco comics dealers. As you predicted, they didn't ask any questions about how we came by them."

"Everything is going very well."

"Yes, except . . . never mind."

"What? You still have the feeling your brother is alive?"

"It may just be that I'm wishing Shawn was alive."

"Might be a good idea to forget all about that, Sally."

"The way you've forgotten all about your wife?"

"Yeah, exactly."

"What's her name?"

"There's no reason to—"

"If you aren't brooding about her running off and aren't deeply hurt inside—you ought to be able to say her name aloud."

He considered that while looking out at the calm Pacific. "All right. Her name is Betsy."

Sally laughed. "That's an awfully dippy name."

"No dippier than Sally."

"Sure, it is. Sally has class and style. Betsy is what you name your puppy—or a horse. 'Whoa there, Betsy.' Or maybe a cow—'Time for the milkin', Betsy.'"

He nodded, kept looking out to sea.

She took hold of his hand. "I love you, by the way."

"So I've heard." He turned, took hold of her and kissed her.

After a moment she said, "One more bit of business. Have you phoned any new *Freddie Foible* ideas to Wally?"

"I phoned him," he answered. "Told him we'd be sending him his percentage of the take. And—I quit the strip."

She pressed her hands together and smiled at him. "That's great," she said. "And now will you try to sell a comic strip of your own?"

"Yeah, I've already been making some notes and sketches."

"What's it about?"

"What do you think?"

"Cockroaches," she said.

"Cockroaches," he said.